The Fifth Favorite

For Aleene,

Stand in the
love of the Lord!!

Gale Sears

The Fifth Favorite

Gale Sears

CrossLink Publishing

CrossLink Publishing
1601 Mt. Rushmore Rd, STE 3288
Rapid City, SD 57702

Ordering Information:
Quantity sales. Special discounts are available on quantity purchases by corporations, associations, and others. For details, contact the "Special Sales Department" at the address above.

The Fifth Favorite/Sears —1st ed.

ISBN 978-1-63357-185-3

Library of Congress Control Number: 2019944253

First edition: 10 9 8 7 6 5 4 3 2 1

Scripture quotations marked "KJV" are taken from the Holy Bible, King James Version (Public Domain).

To my mom and dad, whom I honor.

Chapter One

Allie Whitman knew that some things were better left alone: a black widow spider on the woodpile, a snarling dog behind a chain-link fence, and definitely the madwoman of Tahoe Meadow.

Allie didn't have anything to do with the madwoman for eleven years of her life. She only knew about her through whispered stories from her friends at slumber parties, and snatches of conversation from the gossips of the town. Rumor had it the madwoman liked to kill small animals and bury them in her backyard. Mrs. Culp, her mom's hairdresser, said she'd heard that the madwoman cut off the heads of the poor little things and placed them on sharp poles to mark the gravesites. Mr. Coleman, owner of the Blue Bell Café, said the madwoman lived like a hermit in her decaying old house, with no electricity, and only a mangy, mean dog for company.

Allie was a smart girl, so she didn't go anywhere near the madwoman's house at the end of Tallac Road—that was until her mom got a bee in her bonnet to have the madwoman do some of the family laundry. Every Monday, her mom loaded up two laundry baskets with Dad and Paul's white shirts, the Sunday tablecloth, Allie and Stephanie's better cotton dresses, and her little sister Trudy's everyday clothes. Trudy's clothes had to be done a certain way or the eight-year-old wouldn't put them on. Trudy had some weird problems that no one really understood. Allie tried mostly to ignore her. In fact, Allie was perfectly content to steer clear of anything weird or unpleasant, so when her mom decided that she was taking laundry to the madwoman's house and that Allie was coming along, she put her foot down. She stated flatly that it was a nutty idea, and that she would not be going. That strategy had not worked out so well.

Allie knew that her mom was different from other moms. Yes, indeed, her mom certainly had her own way of thinking about a lot of things: She liked *I Love Lucy*, but she didn't *love* it like the other two million Americans who had television sets; she wore slacks and capri pants to parent-teacher conferences (which Allie found mortifying); and two months ago, she'd started talking with the neighbors about starting a relief group to help the starving kids in China. This last thing made her dad wonder a bit, but all he said was, "China's a long way away, Patricia."

Allie thought her dad should have been mortified or rankled at the idea, but he took it with his normal smile, sigh, and shake of his head. Allie knew that *she* would have been rankled. *Rankled.* That was a great word. She kept a list of great words in the back of her diary. One day she was going to work for a newspaper and travel around the world writing stories and using all her great words. But today was Monday, and as Allie pulled her hair back into a ponytail, she felt like there was a wad of yellow rubber bands in her stomach. After school, she'd be trudging after her mom to the madwoman's house with a basket of dirty clothes. It was their third Monday doing this, and Allie's only hope was that her mom wouldn't catch on to the trick she'd used the other two visits. She'd quickly put her basket next to the old rusted screen door, then hurried back to sit on the creaking wooden stairs, pretending to tie her shoe. And it had worked! She didn't have to see the old lady's face or risk catching sight of any sawed-off animal heads. Allie made a face in the mirror as she felt her stomach twist again. Great! She probably wouldn't be able to eat any breakfast this morning.

* * *

"Mom, I think Allie's turning into a cat," her brother, Paul, said as he slid into his seat next to her at the breakfast table.

Allie sat straighter and narrowed her eyes.

"She was just about to lap up her Rice Krispies directly from the bowl."

Mrs. Whitman gave him one of her looks. "Well, son of mine, there's the pot calling the kettle black." She plunked down a plate of toast in the center of the table and pulled Paul's ear. "When you were her age, we never even gave you silverware."

Allie laughed, and Paul laughed with her.

"Was I really ever eleven?" He shuddered dramatically. "Actually, I think I went straight from ten to seventeen."

"Actually, you didn't," Mom said bluntly. "It would have been nice, but...no." She looked at the clock. "Stephanie! Breakfast is on the table!"

Trudy piped up from her small table in the corner of the kitchen. "The barometric pressure is rising."

Mom went over to her and gently placed her index finger on the old, weathered barometer. "Thank you for the update, Tru."

"That's the way it goes."

Paul laughed. "Tru, you crack me up."

"I would never do that."

Paul laughed harder.

Mom moved to the hall doorway. "Stephanie, breakfast!"

"Okay! Okay!" came a growling voice from the back bedroom. "I can't get my hair to go right!"

"Maybe it wants to go left!" Paul called to her.

"Shut up, Paul!"

"Stephanie."

"Sorry, Mom. Be quiet, Knucklehead!"

Mrs. Whitman sighed and shook her head. No smile.

"I *know* I was never fifteen," Paul said, shoving half a piece of toast into his mouth all at once.

"Yes, you were. That was the year you broke your arm sledding at Hope Valley. I have pictures."

Allie chuckled. She got a kick out of her mom's picture-taking. Two Christmases ago, their dad had given her a fancy Kodak camera, which she named Gertie. Gertie was an instant success, and the picture-taking began that holiday morning. It was immediately apparent that her mom had her own idea of what made a great photo. She was far keener on photos of people in ugly snow hats, and faces in pain from a broken arm, than people standing around with frozen smiles on their faces. In this one thing, Allie had to agree with her mom. She hated staged photos. She always looked totally goofy. She felt she wasn't so bad-looking when she was a baby and up until about four, but then she turned five and her front teeth started falling out. After that, forget it! It was either ugly glasses, or frizzy hair, or half-closed eyelids. Eight out of ten pictures she looked like she was about to fall over, sneeze, or cry. Her perfect sister Stephanie tried to assure her that she was just going through a gawky stage. Huh! What did she know? She'd never gone through a gawky stage. Even when she had braces at ten and eleven, she somehow pulled it off as cool.

"Stephanie May Whitman!" Mom yelled. "Breakfast! Now!"

"Okay!" came the frustrated answer, followed by the bang of a closet door and the tromp of footfalls in the hallway.

Trudy glanced briefly toward the hallway, then back to her tray, which was neatly stacked with papers. "There will be cumulus clouds this afternoon, with no chance of rain."

"Thank you, Tru," Mom said, handing her a graham cracker. "I will not wear my raincoat or galoshes."

Stephanie came sulking into the kitchen with a glower and a growl as Mom placed a bowl of almonds on the table. Stephanie took a handful and flopped down in her chair.

"Your hair looks awful," Paul teased.

"Shut...shush...be quiet, Paul," Stephanie stammered.

"Your hair looks great," Mom said earnestly. "I wish my hair had that curl."

"This frizz, you mean?"

Allie groaned. Stephanie kind of made everyone sick with how much she talked about herself, especially her looks. She was actually nice-looking with caramel-colored hair in soft curls, blue eyes, and straight teeth. She was also average height with just the right amount of curves for a fifteen-year-old. Allie often wondered what she had to squawk about, especially since she was really smart in school, too—even science.

Last summer, the Whitman family had ventured from Lake Tahoe to San Francisco to visit their Uncle Ed and Aunt Josie. While they were there, they went on a boat ride in the San Francisco Harbor. Mom stayed onshore with Trudy, and not long after the boat set sail, Allie was wishing she'd stayed with them on solid ground. As the boat swayed and rolled on the waves, she became as sick as a dog; Stephanie bounced around the deck, flirting with the deck hands, and asking a million questions about the ocean. The rest of the day, Little Miss Smarty-Pants vowed to become a marine biologist and sail the seas. Allie figured she'd better stop worrying about what her hair looked like with all the wind and sea spray on a boat.

Mom set a bowl of fruit cocktail in front of Stephanie, and a four-egg omelet in front of Paul. He beamed up at her.

"Thanks, Mom. You are the greatest mom in the world."

"Don't forget that the next time I have to ground you." She handed another graham cracker to Trudy.

"Ground me? I never do anything wrong," Paul said through a mouthful of egg.

Mom raised her eyebrows and went back to cooking.

Allie sat staring at her big brother, admiring his ability to eat a half a piece of toast all at once. Paul took after their mom, tall and lanky. Stephanie and Trudy were a mix of Mom and Dad, and

Allie was all Dad—short and sturdy. *Sturdy* was her mom's word, and she was always telling Allie not to get too attached to it.

"You're approaching that great age of change. I'll look at you in a couple of years and won't recognize you, except for your eye color."

Allie didn't find that very comforting, as her eyes were just kind of blah blue.

"Mom, I have science club after school," Stephanie said.

Her sister's announcement brought Allie back to the breakfast table. She scowled over at her, jealous of her brain.

"I remember. I'll pick you up at five." Mom moved the toast away from Paul and set the jar of peanut butter by Allie's plate.

"Are you coming in Dad's car?"

Allie scooted her chair a little farther away from her sister and busied herself with putting peanut butter on her toast. She watched as her mom turned slowly and put a hand on her hip.

"Now, why would I come in Dad's car?"

Stephanie gulped down a mouthful of fruit cocktail. "Um...I...I just thought..."

"You just thought you'd be embarrassed by my plain gray Ford sedan with the crunched-up rear bumper?"

"No...I..."

"No? Then it must be that you're concerned for my welfare driving such an old car."

"Well, ...it's just that..."

Mother put on her soft eyes. "I knew it had to be something like that, little sweetheart. I knew it couldn't be anything shallow or silly like worrying about what the other kids at school might think of you. You have much too much character for that." Mom smiled. "Would you like more fruit?"

"No, I'm good."

Mom turned back to the stove. "Yes, you are good."

Allie started to giggle, but she decided against it when she saw Stephanie's murderous look.

Paul leaned over to Stephanie and whispered, "Hey, you take the school bus. That's pretty uncool."

"A lot of kids take the bus in the fall and winter," she answered with a shrug.

Allie nodded. That was true. Since the middle school occupied a wing of the high school, in the cold months, the bus was filled with kids, from miniscule sixth graders all the way up to sophisticated seniors.

"We all take the bus except for you and your stupid friends who walk every morning."

"Good exercise. You should try it."

Stephanie glared at him. "Why don't *you* try exercising your brain?" Her eyes widened. "Oh sorry, that would take a brain, which you don't have."

Allie decided to change the subject. "Mom, what time did Dad leave for the office?"

"Early," Mom answered, finally sitting down to her English muffin and coffee. "Ah, two minutes of rest."

She always said that. *"Two minutes of rest."* Allie supposed it was because that's what she got—two minutes of rest at a time.

"But his car is still in the driveway," Stephanie inserted.

"And there it will remain," Mom said, giving her a knowing smile. "He walked to work today. He said it was such a beautiful autumn morning that he wanted to be out enjoying it."

Allie and Paul laughed. They knew he walked because Mom told him to get some exercise. Not that their dad was chubby or anything; it was just that he had a lot of stress from being a CPA, and Mom insisted that exercise helped him to calm down.

Mom turned to Allie. "We go to Mrs. Hemmett's today."

Allie grimaced. "Horrible Hemmett's," she mumbled.

Paul laughed. Usually it was the thing Allie liked best about her brother—his easy laugh—but not now. Not when she was in danger of decapitation by a madwoman.

"Allie?"

"Yes, ma'am?"

Mom glanced over at her as she spread jam on her English muffin. "I will drop Trudy off with Mrs. Rose and then I'll be home to pick you up. So, don't miss the bus."

"On purpose," Paul said.

Allie looked over at him and narrowed her eyes.

He grinned. "Hey! I understand. I wouldn't want to go to her creepy house, either."

"Speaking of the bus, it will be here in about three minutes," her mom said with a flick of her hand toward the clock.

Allie tried to shove the rest of her toast in her mouth like Paul did, but it ended up with her choking and spitting out half-chewed bits of toast onto her plate.

"Gross," Stephanie said, shaking her head. "Mom, can't you do anything about her manners?"

"Good idea. Right after school you can start teaching her."

"No!" both girls shouted together.

"I didn't think so." Mom took another bite of English muffin. "Now, get going or you'll miss the bus." She stood, finished her coffee, and moved toward the sink.

"Cumulus clouds, not to be confused with cumulus congestus, or cumulonimbus," Trudy reported, holding up her drawing.

"Great cloud picture, Tru," Paul said as he passed by her table, grabbing his gym bag and heading for the door. "Bye Mom! Be good today."

Mrs. Whitman pointed at her own eyes with V fingers and then turned them to Paul, which all the kids knew meant, *I've got my eyes on you.*

Paul laughed and bolted out the door. "Keep your curses away from me, witch woman!"

Mrs. Whitman shook her head and smiled as she picked up Paul's plate. It was a nice smile, and Allie wondered if her mom ever looked at her like that. She doubted it. If *she* ever called her mom "witch woman," she'd get a snap with the tea towel.

The bus horn tooted, and Allie jumped from her chair. Mr. Cross, the bus driver, only waited one minute for the late kids to make it to the bus before he drove off. Luckily Allie knew she could make it from the kitchen door to the bus stop in forty-five seconds if there wasn't rain and she had on her Buster Browns. It took sixty seconds if there was rain and she was wearing galoshes, and nearly two minutes if there was snow and she needed snow boots. Today it was Buster Browns, so she would be fine. She threw on her jacket and grabbed her book bag. She was about to follow Stephanie out the door when her mom spoke calmly.

"Lunch."

"Argh!" Allie growled as she ran back to snatch her plaid lunchbox off the counter.

"And glasses."

"Argh!" Allie growled again as she scooped her glasses off the table. There was a splotch of peanut butter on one of the lenses, but she'd clean that when she was on the bus.

"You're welcome," her mother said.

"Thanks!" Allie yelled as she jumped from the back step into a pile of raked aspen leaves. She kicked her way through, enjoying the crunchy swooshing sounds she was making. She came out onto the dirt path and started running, managing to make it to the bus way ahead of Stephanie. Of course, Stephanie would never run for the bus, and of course Mr. Cross would wait for her even if it added minutes to his route.

"Morning, Allie!" Mr. Cross said cheerily. "Nice sprint."

Allie took a deep breath and nodded. "Thanks." She made her way to the seat she and her friend Frances always shared.

"Hi, Allie!" Frances called, giving her the classic Frances wave—hand stationary, fingers wiggling.

"Hi, Frances! What's your tale, Nightingale?"

"What's the story, Morning Glory? You were almost late."

"Yep. Mom took forever to get breakfast on the table today," Allie said, flopping into her seat.

"Morning, Miss Stephanie," Mr. Cross said, as Stephanie climbed slowly onto the bus.

Stephanie adjusted her book bag. "Hi, Mr. Cross. How's your son doing?"

"Oh, good, good. Thanks for asking. Got his leg in a cast. Won't be doing any skiing this season."

"That's too bad. He's Olympic material, if you ask me."

"Yep, yep. True enough. Thanks for saying so."

Allie stared at her sister as she made her way down the aisle to an empty seat at the back of the bus. "What was that all about?" Allie whispered to Frances. "I didn't even know Mr. Cross had a son."

Frances shrugged. "Me neither."

The bus started rolling, and Frances pulled a book out of her school bag.

"What ya doing?"

"I'm not ready for the math test today."

Allie got a sudden pain in her stomach. "Math test? I forgot! Oh, man! Let me study with you."

"Sure. Don't worry. I think it's only times tables."

Great, Allie thought. *A times tables test and a trip to Horrible Hemmett's. This is not going to be a good day.*

Chapter Two

There was blood on the rusted screen door. Old dried blood, or brown gravy. Maybe it was mud. Allie tried not to look at it, but she couldn't stop her eyes from jumping from the dirty clothes in her clothes basket to the gross screen door coming closer and closer every second. Maybe somebody had spilled brown paint. Her mother reached out and knocked— right on the bloody spot! Allie raced forward, plunked down her basket, and turned to hurry back to the stairs.

"Stay with me," her mother said.

"But my shoelace..."

"Stay here."

"Mom, I..."

"Stay."

Allie turned, just as the front door screeched open.

"Good afternoon, Mrs. Hemmett," her mom said, as though she was talking with her hairdresser.

"Mrs. Whitman," came the gruff answer. There was a long pause. "Is that your daughter?"

Allie felt her stomach flip when those words came out of Horrible Hemmett's mouth. She stared harder at her shoes. Hey! Her shoelace really was untied!

"Yes. This is my daughter Allie. Allie, say hello to Mrs. Hemmett."

I can't because then I'll have to look up and see her bloody door and madwoman face.

"Allie, mind your manners."

"Hi, Mrs. Hemmett. Nice day." She glanced up quickly and was relieved that she couldn't see much of anything through the rusted screen door. Just some gray-colored hair and a white apron.

"Matter of opinion," Mrs. Hemmett said. She held the screen door open with her hip and reached out for the basket of laundry. Her mom handed it over.

"Allie, bring yours over now."

"Mom, I..."

"Just grab it and hand it to me," her mom said in a forced light voice that actually meant *Do it now, or else.*

Allie picked up the basket and took it to her mom. While handing it over, she made the mistake of looking at Mrs. Hemmett. *Ah!* This was worse than seeing something gross on the screen door or cut-off animal heads on spikes! This was a face from a nightmare. *Horrific!* That was the word Allie would write today in the back of her diary. Horrific! She stared. She couldn't stop herself—she couldn't stop looking at the blotchy, lumpy skin with scars running around the nose and underneath one eye. And then, Allie realized that the scar eye was looking right at her! She stepped back.

Mrs. Hemmett took a deep breath and turned her gaze on Allie's mom. Slowly she took the basket from her hands. "Didn't tell her what to expect?" Mom didn't answer. "Well, that was damn stupid of you." She let the rusted screen door close. "See you on Thursday for pickup." She shoved the front door closed with her foot. It banged, and Allie jumped.

"Come on, let's go," her mom said gruffly.

"Mom?" Allie asked turning slowly from the door. She discovered her mom was already halfway down the rickety wooden stairs. She ran to follow. "Mom! What the heck was that?"

"Never mind."

Allie persisted. "What the heck..."

"Don't use that word."

"What was that? What was wrong with Mrs. Hemmett's face?"

Her mom didn't answer. She didn't answer on the way home, either. In fact, Allie was dropped off at Frances's house, which was fine with her. Her mom said she had an errand to run before picking up Stephanie and Trudy, and that Allie was to be home in time for dinner. Her mom had a look on her face like when Mr. Mathews, the butcher, charged her too much for ground beef. Yeah, that was the look—only worse.

* * *

There weren't enough chocolate chip cookies in the world to make her stomach settle down at the thought of Mrs. Hemmett's face, but Frances pushed the plate toward her, so Allie grabbed another and shoved it in her mouth.

"And she called your mom stupid?"

"Well, she said it was "blank" stupid for Mom not to tell me about what her face looked like ahead of time. As if it would make any difference. Nothing could get you ready for something like that."

"But you knew her face was awful. Everybody talks about it all the time."

"Yeah, they talk about it." Allie stood and imitated some of the adult conversations she'd heard. "Horrible Hemmett? Well, she certainly doesn't need a mask for Halloween, that's for sure. Horrible Hemmett? Now, that's a face only a mother could love. Poor Mabel Hemmett. Shame about her face. Tragic shame." She sat down and took another cookie. "They say stuff like that, but they don't say *exactly* what it looks like. Not that blotchy old blob of skin."

Frances shuddered like somebody had poured cold water down her back. "And it was like stitches in her skin like that Frankenstein monster?"

"The Frankenstein monster? How'd your parents let you watch that movie?"

"They didn't know I was watching. We were at the drive-in and they thought I was asleep in the back of the station wagon."

"Nifty."

Frances did a handstand against the wall. "So, now what are ya gonna do the next time you have to go there?"

"I'm not."

"Not, what?"

"I'm not going there again."

"How ya gonna get outta that?"

"I'll just tell my mom I'm not going."

Frances grunted and flipped her feet away from the wall. "Fat chance."

"Besides, I bet my mom is going to fire Mrs. Hemmett from doing our laundry, 'cause she cussed at her. So, I won't have to worry about it." Allie lay back on the bed. "Ugh. My stomach hurts."

"Well, no wonder. You ate almost the whole plate of cookies."

Just then Frances's mother called up the stairs. "Frances? Time for Allie to run along home. Dinnertime."

Allie groaned. "I have rocks in my stomach, and I think Mom's cooking meatloaf tonight." She rolled over and slid off the bed. "Maybe I can sneak some of my dad's Alka-Seltzer."

Frances walked with her to the front door, where Frances's mother was waiting. When Allie looked up at her, she put on a mom smile. "Glad you could come and play, Allie."

"And work on our science project," Frances reminded.

"Of course, and work on your science project," Mrs. Catera added, smiling again. "Walk home carefully."

"I will, Mrs. Catera. Thanks for the cookies."

"I'll walk you to the gate," Frances said as she followed Allie out the door.

"Oh... well, alright," Mrs. Catera said with hesitation. "But don't be too long. Dinner in five minutes."

"It's just the front gate, Mom. It's not China," Frances said.

"Don't be sassy," her mother scolded.

"Sorry, Mom."

The girls ambled out to the gate. A bird was warbling away in the neighbor's bare-branched lilac bush—the sound making Allie sigh. "It'll be winter soon."

"Don't say that. We've still got Halloween and maybe part of November before snow."

"Fat chance."

"Well, we've still got till Halloween," Frances insisted.

"Maybe."

"Thought about what you're gonna be?"

"Nope. You?"

"My mom wants me to be Little Bo Peep," Frances said with a grimace.

"Yuck."

"I know." She opened the gate. "My dad wants me to be Lucille Ball."

"Your parents are weird."

Frances looked quickly to the door of her house. "I know, right?"

"Don't worry. Mine are weird, too."

Just then the door opened. "Frances, dinner!" Mrs. Catera said in a cheerful voice.

"Okay, coming!" Frances answered in *her* cheerful voice. She turned to go, then turned back. "Remember to bring the pipe cleaners and the duct tape for our science project tomorrow."

"Yep. I won't forget."

"See ya later, alligator."

"After a while, crocodile." Allie waved and started off down the road. The sky was still pale with color, and she knew she'd make it home before dark. It was only four blocks. The bird was still warbling in the lilac bush, and to Allie's mind he seemed to be saying, *"Don't worry, you won't be going back. Don't worry, you won't be going back."*

She stepped out onto the road and heard the squeal of a car coming around the corner of Stanford Avenue. The car lights were on, and they shone right into her eyes. *Stupid driver.* "Watch where you're going!" she yelled.

"Stay out of the street!" a young male voice called as the car sped by.

"Punk! Stupid punk!" Allie shouted in her meanest I-hate-you voice.

"Hey, your sister's a tough girl," were the words that came back at her. Then voices laughing.

Allie squinted at the retreating car. *Was Paul in that car?* There was a tall boy in the passenger seat with short, cropped hair, but all of Paul's friends had short, cropped hair. They were the cool guys in high school. *Were Paul and his cool friends laughing at her?*

By the time Allie made it home, she was ready to kick something and cry at the same time. Even the warm glow of the house light didn't make her feel better, and the sound of arguing voices when she got to the front porch made her catch her breath. She stood with her hand on the doorknob. She was just about to go around to the back when the front door was wrenched open.

"There you are," her mother snapped.

"I...I heard arguing."

"Well, never mind. Go wash up for dinner."

"But I..."

"Go wash your hands."

Allie slid past her mother and caught a glimpse of Paul's legs as he took the stairs two at a time toward his bedroom.

"Paul, were you in a car..."

"Not now, squirt."

"But I think one of your friends..."

The bedroom door slammed.

Trudy started wailing from the kitchen, and Mrs. Whitman went to calm her.

"Hey there, Allie," her dad said from his front room chair.

Allie went to join him. "What's up?" she asked, plopping down on his ottoman.

"Rent's up, from what I hear."

"Dad. No, really. Why's everybody mad?"

"Angry."

"Okay, angry. Why?"

"I think your brother was riding around in a car with someone reprehensible."

Allie brightened. "Good word! What's it mean?"

"Someone your mother doesn't like."

"Yeah? Well, I don't like him much, either. Stupid cool guy almost ran me down over on Stanford Avenue."

Her dad sobered. "Really? Are you hurt?"

"No, no! Nothing big. Just scared me a little." Allie was sorry she'd said anything, because now her dad's face was looking all grumpy and serious.

"Really, Dad, no big deal."

He stood up. "Maybe I should talk with your mother."

"Hey, it was nothing." She jumped up and did a spin in front of him. "Really! See? I'm fine. Anyway, it's dinner and Mom's very busy..."

"Dinner's ready!" came the call from the kitchen.

"See? I told ya. Anyway, I don't want her any more mad—angry—with Paul."

Mrs. Whitman came to the front room door. "Alan, did you hear me? It's time for dinner."

"Yes, we're coming." He put his hand on Allie's shoulder as they walked to the kitchen. "You're sure you don't want me to say anything?"

"Definitely. Sometimes it's just better to keep the peace."

Her dad chuckled. "Hey! That's my line."

Allie slid into her seat. "I know, and it's a good one."

Mother turned from the counter and set the plate of meatloaf on the lazy Susan. "What's a good one?"

"Your meatloaf!" Allie said brightly. "I'm so hungry I could eat a horse."

Trudy gasped. "No! No! Don't eat a horse! Don't eat a horse!"

Allie turned toward her table in the corner. "It's okay, Tru. I'd never do that. I'm gonna eat some of Mom's yummy meatloaf."

"Stephanie! Dinner!" Mom called.

Allie prayed that Stephanie would come quickly to the table, and not have some smart remark that would start more fireworks. Just as she started to worry that Mom would have to call her again, Stephanie magically appeared.

"Sorry, Mom. I had to finish my last algebra problem." Allie stared at her in disbelief, and Stephanie glared back. "What's your problem?" she whispered as Mom went to get the green beans.

"Well, it's not algebra, that's for sure."

Stephanie ignored her. "Where's Paul?"

Allie slouched down in her chair as Mom reached over her and put the green beans on the lazy Susan. "I guess he's decided to skip dinner."

"What? He never skips dinner."

"Patricia, do you remember what night we told the Taylors we'd play bridge?" Dad asked suddenly.

"For heaven's sake, Alan, Friday like always."

"Oh, yeah. That's right. You know, I think I'll wear that new dress shirt you bought me."

Mom set the mashed potatoes on the lazy Susan and sat down. "Really? I thought you didn't like it."

"No, actually I do. I just had to get used to the color. Yellow's a little different."

Allie noticed a slight smile at the corner of her mom's mouth.

"Well, I suppose so when all you ever wear is white, blue, or gray."

Dad laughed. "That's not true. I have a few brown things, too."

Mom laughed.

Crisis averted, Allie thought as she took the bowl of mashed potatoes and scooped out a glob. It kind of reminded her of Mrs.

Hemmett's face, and she quickly smashed the potatoes flat. She looked up to see Stephanie staring at her.

"You are very weird, little sister."

Allie handed her the bowl. "I know, but weird is better than being a know-it-all."

"Allie," her mom said in that slow warning voice that Allie knew well.

"Sorry, Mom." She smiled sweetly at her sister. "Here, Steph. Would you care for some green beans?"

"Oh, give it up, little sis."

Allie winked at her, then concentrated on taking the smallest piece of meatloaf she could find. *Reprehensible.* Later she'd be looking up that word in her dictionary and writing it in the back of her diary. She'd also be writing in her daily notes about Mrs. Hemmett's gruesome face, and how much she hated stupid teenage boys—especially stupid teenage boys who tried to run her over with their stupid cars.

Chapter Three

Mr. Nessen stood staring at the wad of duct tape in Allie's hand. She continued to scrunch the silver gob into a ball shape, feeling less and less sure about the project she and Frances had picked for the science fair. She took a quick peek at Mr. Nessen's face. He did not look happy.

"I thought you girls were doing a tribute to NASA."

"We are!" Frances said brightly. "For their third anniversary. See? Allie's making *Sputnik*!"

"The first orbiting satellite launched by the Russians," Mr. Nessen said, emphasizing the word *Russians*.

"Well, there was the dog, and we wanted to put the dog in it," Allie offered, holding up the small plastic dog that would be shoved into the duct tape satellite.

Their science teacher took the wad and tossed it into the air several times. "Which was *Sputnik II,* also launched by the Russians."

"Ah...well, we know, but..."

"But we're also gonna do *Explorer I,*" Frances said quickly.

Mr. Nessen stopped tossing. "Well, finally something American."

"Oh sure," Frances continued. "First American satellite! We're gonna do that and talk about Mr. Von Brown."

"Von Braun."

"Huh?"

"Wernher von Braun. The name of the scientist who was the head of the Explorer project."

"Right! We love him," Allie chimed in. "We're going to talk all about him, and the start of NASA, and President Eisenhower."

Mr. Nessen handed back the duct tape ball and gave the girls a serious look. "You two have a lot of work to do."

"Yes, sir," they chorused.

"And your satellite is not impressive. Figure out a different construction."

"Yikes," Allie said as Mr. Nessen walked away. "What happened to Nice Guy Nessen?"

"Maybe he has indigestion or something," Frances growled, grabbing the *Sputnik* model and tossing it into the wastebasket.

"Yeah," came a laughing whisper behind the girls. "He took one look at your lame project and wanted to puke."

Allie spun around in her chair. "Shut up, Todd Fisher!"

"Miss Whitman!"

Allie turned back to see the frowning face of Mr. Nessen. "Yes, sir?" she answered in her most innocent voice.

"We are not to use such language, are we?"

"No, sir, but..."

"You will stay in at recess and write a hundred lines—*I must be the master of my tongue.*"

Todd Fisher guffawed into his hand, as his friend Sam leaned forward.

"Wow, Bowling Alley, you just got a gutter ball."

Frances turned to glare at him. She turned back to Allie. "Sorry."

Allie shrugged. "Not your fault."

"But I picked NASA. We probably should have gone with your idea about dinosaurs."

Allie brightened. "We still could, ya know."

"The baby dinosaur skeleton?"

"Yeah! I know right where Trudy's dead hamster is buried."

Frances shuddered. "But digging up a dead animal? It's why I didn't want to do it before. It'll be all gooey and gross."

"I don't think it will. It died years ago, so it should only be bones." Frances hesitated. "I'll dig it up myself—you won't even need to be there."

"Well...okay."

"Super! And you can find cool pictures of people digging up dinosaurs in your dad's *National Geographic.*"

Frances nodded. "I could do that. And I could make a big pretend dinosaur bone out of plaster of paris."

"See! It'll be fun!"

"But won't your mom be mad at you for digging up Trudy's pet?"

Allie hesitated. "Yeah, she would, but I'm not going to tell her."

"You're not?"

"No. And nobody's going to see me, 'cause I'll be very sneaky."

"But..."

"And we'll put it together at your house." Allie waited while Frances's face went through several anxious expressions. "Come on, Frances. Just think how proud our moms will be when we bring home the highest mark in the class."

"Okay, okay. I guess it'll be cool."

"Very cool!"

The bell rang for recess, and all the students stood, noisily heading for the equipment closet. Frances went to retrieve a four-square ball, returning to stand by Allie's desk as she got out her pencils and paper.

"Sorry, you have to do lines."

"Well, I must be the master of my tongue."

The girls laughed.

"It won't be fun playing four-square without you."

"Get Sharon Smith to play."

"Very funny; all she wants to do is talk to the boys."

"Miss Catera, leave Miss Whitman to her work."

"Yes, Mr. Nessen." Frances gave Allie a thumbs-up and headed out the door.

"Dinosaurs! Much better than orbiting space stuff," Allie mumbled to herself. She was thinking about what shovel she'd use for digging up Mr. Stubbs, as she wrote:

I must be the master of my tongue.

I must be the master of my tongue.

Chapter Four

Their little camping shovel was just the right size. It was easy to carry, and the scoop didn't pick up too much dirt at one time. Even though it was getting dark, Allie forced herself not to hurry. She carefully shoved the blade into the ground and brought up a shovel full of dirt. She didn't want to smash into the bones, and she figured if the body of Mr. Stubbs was disintegrated, then his cardboard coffin would be dust, too. She dumped the dirt onto the pile and calculated again the position of the burial—straight across from the corner of the shed, between the two small pine trees, the one with a scar on its side where she'd first learned to use a hatchet. Allie quickly scratched that memory from her mind. Even Dad was angry with her for that goofball act.

Allie glanced around to make sure she was alone. She'd be glad when the dinosaur double was safely housed in the tin cracker box she'd brought, the grave filled in, and the shovel returned to the shed. There were several pine trees and bushes between her and the back of the house, so she was fairly sure she wouldn't be discovered, but she would breathe a lot easier when this particular adventure was over.

She brought up another load of dirt and noticed small flecks of pinkish paper in the mix. She shined her Girl Scout flashlight on it to be sure. This was it! Her mom had put Mr. Stubbs in a red shoebox and let Trudy carry the coffin to the graveside. The color probably got washed out from being in the ground for so long. Allie shivered. What *would* Mr. Stubbs look like: bits of guts and brown fur bleached out to white? She swallowed several times and blew out a puff of air. As she reached into the hole, her brain kept thinking: *paleontologist, paleontologist, paleontologist.*

She just had to think of herself as a scientist. *Hey! I even brought along a paintbrush to swipe the dirt off the bones.* Allie shined her flashlight into the hole and carefully loosened the dirt from the flecks of crumbled shoebox. On the day of the burial, Allie had tried to fake a toothache so she wouldn't have to attend, but Mom had insisted the whole family participate in the rodent funeral: Paul dug the grave, Stephanie played a death march on her recorder (which sounded more like some country-western song), Allie carried a box of tissues in case anyone cried, and Dad held a black umbrella over Trudy's head as she carried the little red cardboard coffin to the grave. Allie remembered how serious Tru was, walking with slow and measured steps. No tears, just slow walking. She was sure her little sister would start screaming or something, but no...just slow walking to the graveside, where she quietly handed over the box to Mom, who deposited it in the hole. The next part was weird: Tru held up her hand like a policeman at a traffic stop and began asking questions. Would Mr. Stubbs be Grandma's pet in heaven? What would he eat? Would he have to be in a cage, or could he just run around on the clouds? Was there a city in heaven for hamsters? Did it hurt when he went to sleep forever? And later, while Mom served everybody lemonade and peach cobbler, Trudy sat down at her desk and started drawing pictures of Mr. Stubbs in heaven—dozens and dozens of pictures of Mr. Stubbs running around on the clouds with other hamsters and eating corn on the cob. After a few months, she just drew clouds. All kinds of clouds.

Something poked her finger, and Allie snatched back her hand. Images flashed in her brain of dreadful things like potato bugs or scorpions. "Don't be stupid," she whispered to herself. "We don't have scorpions in Tahoe." Slowly she peered into the hole and shined her flashlight. Appearing out of the dark dirt was a tiny claw with pointed fingers, and several curved bones close together. Allie fumbled to get her paintbrush out of her pocket. She reached in to clear away the dirt and uncovered Mr. Stubbs's ribs attached to his backbone. *Wow,* she thought. *No skin or anything. Cool.* She cleaned the leg and was just about to uncover the rodent's tiny head when she heard a car pulling into their back neighbor's dirt driveway. Allie turned off her flashlight and lay flat against the ground. *That's weird,* she thought. *The Gibbs family is our summer neighbor, and they shut up their cabin weeks ago.*

The residential area of Al Tahoe was a kid's paradise. The roads were mostly dirt and there were no fences between houses, which meant you could take shortcuts across people's yards any time you wanted, especially since most of the summer cabins were empty once the school year started. But even the part-time neighbors would just wave and ask how things were going when you zoomed by on your bike.

Allie lay flatter and prayed. *Please just have someone using the driveway for a turnaround.* But the driver of the car shut off the engine, and then she heard a car door open and the sound of whispered voices. Allie tried to take little breaths to keep quiet, but that only made her head swim. The car door slammed, and the car backed out of the drive. Then footsteps—coming her way! Allie closed her eyes. *Maybe they won't see me.*

"Allie?" a voice said in a startled whisper.

"Paul?" Allie opened her eyes and let out the breath she was holding. "What the heck are *you* doing?"

"Me?" Paul hissed, ducking down behind the bushes. "What the heck are you doing?"

"I asked you first."

They were both using their "whisper in church" voices.

"Looks like you're graverobbing."

"Don't be stupid! There's nothing to rob from a hamster."

Paul stifled a laugh. "Then what?"

"Then nothing. It's none of your business."

"Nice attitude, little sis." He started to stand. "Well, it might be Mom's business."

"Yeah? Well, it might be Mom's business to know that you rode home with that stupid punk friend of yours who almost ran me over."

Paul slouched back onto his knees. "Oh, he did not."

"I was the one in the road!" Allie hissed. "And then you guys laughed about it."

Paul got serious. "Okay. Let's make a deal. You shut up about me being with Mike..."

"Oooh, so that's the name of the delinquent..."

"And...I won't tell her about you digging up Tru's little pet."

Allie sat up. "You...you wouldn't really tell, would you?"

Paul grinned. "Seems like we both have something we want to keep secret." He held out his hand. "So, do we have a deal?"

Allie narrowed her eyes as she took his hand. "Okay, but tell that reprehensible friend of yours to lay off the gas pedal."

"Wow! *Reprehensible*. Big word, little sister."

Allie got back down on her tummy. "Duh, I'm not six, ya know."

Paul glanced at the house as the side door opened. He crouched lower behind the bushes as their mom stepped out. She cupped her hands around her mouth and hollered, "Allie! Dinner in ten minutes!" She went back inside.

"Did she see us?" Allie whispered in a panic.

"No, she was looking the other way."

"Whew, that was close." Allie anxiously started moving dirt from around the bones. "Shoot! I'll never get this done before we have to go in."

"Hey, hey, careful," Paul warned. "You're gonna break it up." He grabbed the camping shovel. "Here, let me help."

"Really?"

"Sure, we're pals in this, aren't we?" Allie sat back and nodded. "What are you doing with these bones, anyway?"

"Well, if you must know, Frances and I are doing a presentation on dinosaurs for the science fair."

"Pretty tiny dinosaur," Paul said as he carefully scooped underneath the fragile skeleton.

"Well, we're going to put a small plastic army guy next to him, so he'll look gargantuan. It's all about scale, right?"

Paul chuckled. "Oh sure, it's all about scale." He lifted the scoop out of the hole, and Allie shined her light on it.

"I think you got it all!"

"You should hire me full-time."

"Funny. As if I'm going to go around digging up bones all my life."

Paul was gently lifting the skeleton out of the soil along with bits of paper. "Ya never know. Once it gets in your blood—" A wicked grin planted itself on his lips. "Hey! When you go with Mom to Horrible Hemmett's, you should ask if you could dig up all the animals in her pet cemetery."

"Very funny," Allie said, grabbing the cracker tin. "Here, lay him in here. Oh, shoot, one of his arms came off."

"You can just glue that back on, right?"

"Oh...sure. Any good paleontologist knows how to do that."

Paul laid the bones in the tin, and Allie closed the lid with a sigh of relief.

"Thanks, Paul."

"No problem. So, how *are* you gonna keep it a secret from Mom?"

"We're putting him together at Frances's house."

"Smart thinking." Paul held out his hand again for a shake, and Allie took it. "Partners in crime."

Allie gave her brother a slight grin, but inside she wasn't grinning. In fact, she felt like she was about to walk the balance beam in Miss Strum's PE class. She took a deep breath and shook his hand. "Okay. Sure, partners in crime."

Paul winked at her. "Great, you sneak Skeleton Stubbs into the house, and I'll fill in the grave and put the shovel away."

Allie nodded and took off the long way around the house to avoid the kitchen window. She hid the cracker tin behind the dying daisy bush and then went banging in through the front door, breathing hard like she'd just run three blocks.

"Hey, Mom! I'm home! Am I late for dinner?"

"No, you're right on time," her mom called from the kitchen. "Wash up. Dinner in two minutes. Tell your dad."

"Okay." She headed for her dad's office, feeling cocky about her sneakiness.

Mom stepped to the door of the kitchen. "Have you seen your brother?"

Allie froze. "Ah, Paul?"

Mom chuckled. "Well, you only have one brother."

"Ah, no. Nope. I haven't seen him. Maybe Coach kept them longer for practice."

"Well, I'm not holding dinner for him." Mom threw the tea towel over her shoulder and gave Allie a "mom" look. "And change your clothes. It looks like you've been crawling around in the dirt."

"What? Oh, yeah. I...I was helping Brenda Brey get her dog out from under their house."

Her mom turned back into the kitchen. "That family. They have more dogs than sense."

Allie stumbled around dramatically like she was going to faint, bumping into Stephanie as she came down the stairs from the upstairs bathroom. "Hey, watch it!"

"Sorry. Faint from hunger."

Stephanie shook her head. "So weird." She moved to the kitchen. "Mom, can I help with anything?"

Allie made a sour face at her sister's back, turning as her dad came from his office. "Dad! Hi, Dad! Dinner."

"Thank you," he said tweaking her nose. "You seem in a good mood."

"Yeah? Well, maybe that's because I am. Yeah, Frances and I are doing this great science project."

"Really? What is it about?"

"It's a secret."

"Ah. It doesn't involve volcanoes, does it?"

Allie made an "are you kidding me?" face. "Ugh! No! That's something a fourth grader would do."

"Dinner in one minute!" Mom called from the kitchen.

"Chicken enchilada night!" Allie said, doing a little salsa dance, and then she raced up the stairs. "Tell Mom I'll be right down! Don't start without me!"

Allie washed her hands and changed her clothes in record time. She was just scooching out her chair and sitting down, when Paul came into the kitchen. Mom gave him a stern look.

"Coach keep you late?"

Paul smiled, pulled out his chair, and sat down. "Nope. I just thought I'd walk Jennifer home after practice."

Wow. He's pretty smooth with the lies, Allie thought.

"Jennifer? Jennifer Green?" Stephanie asked, her eyes going wide.

Paul gave her a big smile. "Yes, if you must know."

"Who's Jennifer Green?" Mom questioned, setting the enchilada pan on the lazy Susan. "I don't know a Green family in Tahoe."

"They're new," Stephanie said, hogging the conversation. "They moved here from Oregon, and she's the smartest girl in the senior class."

Mom frowned. "How do you know that?"

"Mr. Brock made her the president of the science club because she's got an IQ of like 150 or something." She gave Paul a suspicious look. "So, why's she giving you the time of day?"

"Ouch!" He winked at her. "Maybe, unlike you, she wants to date someone popular."

"Well, a high IQ doesn't mean she's smart about relationships."

"Sounds like somebody's jealous," Allie said, impatient for an enchilada.

Stephanie scowled at her, and Paul laughed.

"That's enough," Mom said. "Let's eat before it gets cold."

"Yes!" Allie said, reaching to scoop two enchiladas onto her plate.

"Just one," Mom said. "If there's extras, you may have seconds."

Paul picked up the spatula and gave his mom a charming puppy dog look. "Can I have two, Mom? Please?"

"May I."

"May I?"

"Oh, for heaven's sake. When have you ever eaten less than four?"

Paul gave her a crooked smile, put two on his plate, and handed the plate to his dad. "You and Dad first."

Allie flopped back in her chair and thunked her plate on the table. *Wow, he's laying it on pretty thick*, she thought. *He'd better be careful.* When it came to detecting lies, Allie figured her mom had *more* than a 150 IQ. Allie tried to give Paul a warning look, but he ignored her. Man, he needed to watch his step, because right now he was hiding a big secret. Her stomach flipped. Two big secrets!

Her stomach rumbled with hunger, but with secret skeletons dancing around in her brain, she figured it was going to be hard to choke down even *one* enchilada.

Chapter Five

Another Monday—and Mom was loading the car with the laundry baskets.

"Where have you been?" she barked as Allie came riding into the yard on Stephanie's hand-me-down Schwinn.

"Playing tether ball with Frances."

"Today is Monday."

Allie skidded to a stop by the side of the car. She straddled her bike and gave her mom a shocked look. "I know it's Monday, but I figured... We're not still going to Horrible Hemmett's, are we?"

"Mind your manners, and yes, we are still going."

"But you didn't say anything at breakfast."

"You know Trudy had a bad morning."

"Yeah, but I thought we weren't going back because Mrs. Hemmett cussed at you last week!"

"Don't be ridiculous. When someone has a rough upbringing, you make allowances."

"What does that mean?"

"Never mind. Put your bike away and hurry."

"But, Mom..."

"Now."

Allie dropped her bike by the front porch, kicked the tire, and mumbled under her breath.

"Stop grumbling," her mom said as Allie came to the car.

Allie pressed her lips together and slid into the passenger's seat, as her mom started the engine and backed out of the driveway.

"You can't make me look at her face again," Allie mumbled.

"I beg your pardon?"

"Nothing."

"Allie Whitman, spit it out!"

"I just wondered, why is her face like that?"

Her mom took a deep breath. "I should have told you before; maybe then you'd have some compassion."

Allie didn't know quite what *compassion* was, but she figured that it meant something about her being able to look at Horrible Hemmett's face and not throw up. She would look it up in her dictionary later tonight. She crossed her arms across her chest and put on her best scowl. "Okay, so?"

"Watch your tone."

"Sorry. So?"

"So, about nine or ten years ago, Mrs. Hemmett was in a bad car accident. Her husband and son were killed. She lived, but her face was badly mangled. The doctor who sewed her up was totally incompetent." Allie figured that meant he didn't know what the heck he was doing. "The Hemmetts pretty much kept to themselves to begin with, but after the accident, Mrs. Hemmett... well, she—"

"Became a hermit," Allie interrupted.

Her mom glanced over at her. "Yes." They were both silent as she turned the car onto Tallac Avenue. "Do you blame her?"

"No." Allie thought about parading that face in public and shivered. She would definitely become a hermit if that was her face. "How'd it happen?"

"The accident?"

"Yeah."

"Yes."

"Sorry, yes—the accident."

"No one knows for sure. The state patrol officer thought Mr. Hemmett might have fallen asleep at the wheel. They went over an embankment and hit a tree."

"Okay, okay. I don't want to hear any more!"

"Fine. Calm down. You need to know the circumstances."

"So I can be compassionate, right?"

"Yes."

"Okay, but I still don't want to look at her face."

They arrived at the house, and her mom shoved the gear shift into park. "Oh, for heaven's sake!" She snapped off the key. "Where did you come from?"

Allie winced. "Well, why don't you just bring Stephanie with you? She's full of compassion."

Her mom got out of the car. "That's why I bring you." She slammed her door and opened the back. "Come get your basket."

Allie moved to the back of the Ford, and her mom handed her the dirty laundry. She trudged along behind, but when they arrived at the screen door she didn't put down her basket or back away. *I'll show her. I'll show her I can be like Stephanie.* Mrs. Whitman knocked on the door and within a few moments, it opened.

Her mom stood up straighter. "Good afternoon, Mabel."

Allie gritted her teeth and looked up. "Afternoon, Mrs. Hemmett."

Mrs. Hemmett looked at her. "Afternoon." She took the basket from Mrs. Whitman and set it inside the door, then came back for Allie's. "It's not polite to stare."

Allie jumped. "Oh! Sorry. Sorry." She handed over the dirty clothes. "It's just that I'd be mad as snot if some doctor did that to me."

Mrs. Hemmett made some sort of croaking sound, and Mrs. Whitman gasped.

"Allie Whitman, what is wrong with you? I'm so sorry, Mrs. Hemmett."

Mabel Hemmett made the croaking sound again, and Allie thought maybe it was some sort of a laugh—a weird laugh—a laugh that hadn't been used in a while. She waited for Mrs. Hemmett to cuss a blue streak, but she just turned back into the house. "See you for pickup." The screen door slammed.

Allie glanced at her mother, who was looking at her as though she was some sort of alien. She stepped forward, took Allie by the shoulder in a grip that was a little bit painful, and headed her toward the car.

"Ow! Mom, ow! I'm sorry. I was just being honest."

"You are grounded for a week!"

"For being honest?'

"For being tactless."

"What's that mean?"

"Look it up. You'll have plenty of time—while you're grounded."

"But, I have to work with Frances on our science project! It's due next Monday!"

"You may do that, but no other activities."

"Ow! Okay! Okay! I get it!" Her mom's grip relaxed, and Allie was grateful that her shoulder wasn't dislocated. She'd had one of those once when she'd fallen off her bike at the meadow, and just remembering that kind of pain made her feel sick.

They both got into the car, and her mom put her hands and her head on the steering wheel. Allie rubbed her shoulder and glared at two kids playing ball in their yard. Finally, her mom took a deep breath and looked up. She looked out the front window at the same two kids Allie was staring at.

"I'm sorry. I didn't mean to hurt you." Allie was silent. "I just don't understand why you can't be more aware of other people's feelings."

"I'm eleven," Allie said sullenly.

Her mother looked over at her. "You will be twelve soon—more than old enough to think before you blurt out the first thing that comes into your head. You need to master your tongue."

Allie jumped. *Man! Had Mr. Nessen snitched on her? Was her mom going to make her write a hundred times—"I must be the master of my tongue"?* She turned and looked at her mom. "Sorry. I'll try."

Her mom nodded. "Okay." She started the car. "Okay. I'm still going to need to tell your father about what you said."

"Do you have to?" Allie asked in a mock worried voice. She knew her dad would give her a stern look, go along with her mother on the punishment, and then sneak a package of rainbow Life Savers into her coat pocket before she left for school.

"Yes. I have to," her mom said, turning the car in the direction of home. "And don't give me that worried look. You know your father is a pushover."

On the ride home, Allie was quiet, but inside, her brain was jumping from Mrs. Hemmett's crazy laugh, to Mom laying her head on the steering wheel, to Dad's pushover face. Just as they were pulling into their driveway, her brain settled on another scary thought. She and Paul had to be careful with their secrets because Mom's "mom antenna" was up on everybody.

Chapter Six

The First Presbyterian Church was one of those places where Trudy was calm, and where her mom didn't wear capri pants. Allie leaned over, looking down the pew and admiring her mom's forest green suit, black high heels, and black pillbox hat. Stephanie caught her not paying attention to the sermon and pointed V fingers at her eyes and then turned them in the direction of the pulpit. Allie stuck out her tongue and sat back in her seat. She scuffed the toes of her Buster Brown shoes back and forth on the worn linoleum and grumbled to herself about being at the end of the row. It was always the same—Mom first, then Trudy, Dad, Stephanie, Paul, and finally her.

Paul reached into his suit pocket and pulled out a piece of white string. "Here, do some cat's cradle and stop fidgeting," he whispered.

"Where'd you get this?" Allie whispered back.

"Shh. Tell ya later."

Allie tied the ends of the string together and started the basic cat's cradle designs. Now that her mind wasn't wandering, she actually heard a few of Pastor Kline's words:

"When the Lord went into the place of the lepers, He did not fear for His life; He did not quake at the sight, He did not shun the disfigured. He reached out His hand—His hand of purity— and laid it on the putrid flesh..."

Allie looked up at the pastor and opened her eyes wide. *Shun? Disfigured? Putrid? Thanks, Pastor Kline. That's a goldmine of new words!* She looked over at Paul and whispered, "What's a leper?"

"Shh." He leaned down. "A person who has leprosy."

"What's that?"

"Some sort of disease where your skin falls off."

"Your skin falls off?" Allie said loudly.

Mother glared over at them, and Paul shrugged his shoulders, pointing at Allie as though it was all her fault. Their mom put her index finger on her lips and glared again. Trudy looked delighted. She clapped her hands and said, "Big mouth."

Allie shot a look at Pastor Kline, and he wasn't smiling. In fact, he was doing his best to ignore the Whitman family completely.

The cat's cradle forgotten, Allie pressed her back against the hard wood of the pew and closed her eyes. She tried to conjure up a picture of a person with their skin falling off, and then of someone touching them. She shuddered and opened her eyes. Who would do that? She studied the stained-glass window of Mary holding the baby Jesus. He was smiling up at His mom, and His one little hand was opened wide, the chubby fingers reaching out. What was Mary thinking, letting Him grow up with the notion that He should go around touching sick people? If *she'd* been Jesus' mom, she would have said, "Now, Jesus, You can go out and be nice to people and teach them wonderful things, but don't touch the people who are sick, because You might get sick, too. And don't make people mad, because they might do terrible things...like kill You." That's what she would have taught Him.

Allie was so caught up in being a better mother to Jesus than Mary she wasn't aware that the sermon had ended until the tones of the benediction hymn started playing.

As they walked slowly down the aisle with the rest of the church crowd, Trudy came up beside her and latched on to the belt of her skirt. "Big mouth," she said.

"Funny." Allie looked around and saw that Stephanie was talking to the bus driver's son. "Hey! I think Stephanie wants you."

"Wants me to what?"

"Wants you to go stand by her."

"Oh, okay," Trudy said, dropping back to stand by her other sister. Stephanie put an arm around her shoulder and continued talking to her friend.

Allie headed for the outside. Even though it was cold, she'd wait for her family by the car. She felt jittery and hungry. She couldn't wait for pot roast and all the fixings. When she finished eating, she was going to spend the whole afternoon at Frances's house finishing their dinosaur project. After a morning filled with leprosy and embarrassment, an afternoon away from her family seemed like heaven.

* * *

"This dinosaur leg bone is perfect!" Allie exclaimed as she held the four-foot-tall bone up in the air. "It looks like a real bone! How'd you do it?"

"My dad helped. It's chicken wire that we covered in newspaper and flour paste."

"It's great! Really great!" Allie set the bone against the wall and stepped back to admire it. "Wow! Mr. Nessen's going to flip when he sees that."

"You think so?"

"Of course, he is."

"Well, he's going to flip over your dinosaur skeleton, too."

Allie moved over to the desk where the bones of Trudy's hamster lay on its side on a *National Geographic* magazine. "Yeah, if I can get it to stand up. We've tried three kinds of glue and nothing works."

Frances put on her thinking face. After several seconds of lip biting and frowning, she brightened. "Hey! How about my mom's clear nail polish? That stuff dries as hard as a rock."

"Good idea!" Allie said. "Let's try it!"

While Frances went off to ask her mother's permission, Allie grabbed Mr. Stubbs's display platform to clean it. Although it was just a small square of plywood, she and Frances had embellished it with pressed autumn leaves, so it looked like the mighty dinosaur was tromping around in the wild. Frances wasn't keen on the idea, and she pointed out that an actual skeleton wouldn't be tromping around anywhere. But Allie liked it, and since this was her major contribution to the project, she had the final say.

When Frances returned with the polish, Allie was at the end of chipping the bits of glue from the board. White paste, Elmer's glue, and rubber cement were finding their way into the trash basket.

"Okay, got it!" Frances said, plopping down at the desk where Allie was working.

"Great! Let's cross our fingers that it works." She took the polish from Frances and applied four globs to the places where Mr. Stubbs paws would be planted.

"Put some on his feet, too," Frances encouraged.

Allie put one on each paw and another on the platform for good measure, while Frances blew on the polish on the stand.

"Why are you doing that?" Allie asked.

"I don't know. My mom told me to. She said the polish should be a little sticky before we put on the skeleton."

"Oh. Okay," Allie said, blowing lightly on Mr. Stubbs's paws.

"Ya think it's ready?" Frances asked.

Allie nodded. "Yeah, let's try it." She gently set the bony feet onto the board.

"Mom said you should hold it there for a while."

"How long is 'a while'?"

Frances shrugged. "A minute or so." She picked up the plastic army man and applied polish to his plastic base. "He's going to look great next to the dinosaur." She dropped some polish onto the board where they hadn't put any leaves. "This is where you want him to stand, right?"

"Yep. Right near his back leg."

"I still think we should have put him lying down underneath one of the front paws. That would have been cool." Frances placed the army man on his spot, holding him in place with one hand and saluting with the other. "Do your duty, soldier! Take down that monster!"

Allie started to laugh, then checked herself as her hand began to shake. "Stop it! Don't make me laugh."

Frances sobered. "Sorry." They were both quiet for a few moments, then Frances sighed and spoke up. "Ya know what I think is cool?"

"What?"

"How your brother helped you dig up the bones."

"Ha! He didn't have much choice."

"What d'ya mean?"

Allie grimaced and then gave Frances a stern look. "Can you keep a secret?"

"Sure. I've still never told anybody about the crush you had on Freddie Vogel last year."

"Yuck. That was stupid, wasn't it? I'm glad he moved to Minnesota." Allie leaned down and studied the skeleton. "You think I should try and let go?"

"Sure, try it," Frances said, a mingled note of excitement and worry in her voice.

Allie took a deep breath, and slowly removed her fingers from the bones. When the skeleton didn't move, she started singing and doing the twist. "Let's twist again like we did last summer. Twist again like we did last year."

Frances let go of her army man and joined her. "Do you remember when things were really hummin'? Twist again, twisting time is here."

"Wahoo! We did it!" Allie yelped.

Frances's mother's voice drifted up the stairs. "Frances, it's getting a little too noisy up there."

Frances ran to the door and opened it to stick her head out. "Sorry, Mom. It's just that the polish worked!"

"Well, I'm glad for that, but you do not need to inform the neighbors."

"Yes, ma'am. We'll be quieter." She came back into the room. "It worked!" she whispered. "It worked; it worked; it worked!"

"Mr. Nessen is definitely going to give us an A," Allie said, beaming at the miniature dinosaur.

The two girls shook hands, laughing and saying things like: *"Good job! Dinosaurs forever! Brilliant science project, an A for sure."*

"And bravo for your brother!" Francis added at the last.

Allie stopped laughing. She had hoped, with all the celebrating, that Frances would forget about Paul. No such luck.

"So, what's the big secret?" Frances asked, plopping onto her bed.

"Ah, it's no big deal. It's just that the evening I dug up Mr. Stubbs, Paul caught me."

"I know, you told me that."

"Well, I didn't tell you that I caught Paul doing something he shouldn't."

"Really? What?"

"He was riding around in a car with that Mike kid."

"So?"

"He's the one who almost ran me down the other week."

"The stupid punk guy?"

"Yeah. My mom can't stand him, and she told Paul he couldn't hang around with him anymore."

"And he still is?"

"Yeah."

"Wow, what's he thinking? Your brother's popular. He doesn't need to pal around with someone like that. Especially after your mom said he couldn't."

Allie shrugged. "Paul said if I keep his secret, then he'll keep my secret."

"My dad says secrets always have a way of seeping out."

"Thanks a lot."

"Not that yours will," Frances said quickly.

"So, should we check and make sure we have everything for tomorrow?" Allie asked abruptly, wishing to change the subject.

"Good idea," Frances said, picking up the huge dinosaur bone and putting it on her bed. "Big dinosaur bone? Check."

"Dino Stubbs? Check."

"Cool display board? Check."

Allie looked everything over. "And you're sure your dad doesn't mind driving all of this stuff to school?"

"It's right on his way to work. He'll just go in a little later than usual."

"Great."

They checked the backdrop board, which was made up of two pieces of cardboard hinged together with duct tape so it would stand on its own in a V shape. It held the paleontology pictures from the *National Geographic* magazine, their handwritten essays on dinosaurs and the profession of being a paleontologist, the timeline of all the eras of dinosaurs from the Triassic, Jurassic, and Cretaceous Periods, and a prehistoric landscape that Frances had painted in the right-hand corner to serve as a background for their little dinosaur.

"Looks good!" Allie said putting on her jacket and mittens. "I'll see you at school tomorrow."

"Roger that," Frances answered, as they raced down the stairs.

They arrived at the front door, and Frances opened it. Allie stopped before stepping outside. "And...make sure your dad carries the dino skeleton, okay?"

"Hey! I'm not clumsy," Frances protested. "I'd be careful with..." She stopped midsentence and gave Allie a sheepish look.

"Yeah, you're probably right. I'll carry the big bone, and Dad can take the other stuff."

"Great!" Allie said, moving out the front gate and picking up her bike.

"Be careful going home!" Frances yelled. "It's kinda dark."

"I'll be fine," Allie shot back. But it *was* dark—a scary Halloween kind of dark with storm clouds overhead and a cold wind moaning through the pine trees. She looked back for Frances's comforting wave, but her friend had already gone back into her house. The bike wobbled when Allie pushed forward. She pressed down on the pedal and tried to get her balance. Her stomach clenched as she fought to keep the bike upright, and after a few frantic moments of pedaling, she had enough speed to keep the bike stable. The cold stung her face and made her eyes water. She reached under her glasses to wipe the tears away, and when her vision cleared, she realized she was headed in the wrong direction.

"Man!" Allie growled. "What a dope!" She started to panic when she realized she was headed down Tallac Avenue toward the meadow—and Horrible Hemmett's house. Her speed increased with the downhill grade of the road, and the bike began to wobble fiercely. She tried to brake, but her foot kept slipping off the pedal. She swerved out into the center of the road and heard the blare of a car horn. She jerked the handlebars to the right and careened off the road into someone's yard, the bike bouncing over pine needles, dirt, and unkempt grass, until it hit a pile of flattened cardboard boxes and stopped short. Allie flew off the bike and hit the ground with a thud, sliding across the granite dirt on her stomach. She felt a sharp pain on her hands and the side of her face, and then—nothing.

Chapter Seven

Her head hurt. Her face hurt. Her hands hurt. Where was she? Allie didn't want to open her eyes. She wanted to believe she was dreaming and that pretty soon she'd wake up. She wanted to believe that, but the pain in her head kept telling her that something terrible had happened. *A car horn? A crash on my bike?*

"Where am I?" *Did she say that out loud?*

"Allie?"

Why is Paul here?

"Allie, can you open your eyes?"

"Don't want to." *What was that strange smell?* She heard Paul chuckle.

"Yep, that's my feisty sister, all right."

"Where am I? Am I home?"

Her brother leaned closer to whisper in her ear. *That strange smell again.* "No, we're at Mrs. Hemmett's place."

Allie's eyes flew open. "What?!" Her head hurt, and she started to cry. "What? Why am I in Mrs. Hemmett's house?" She struggled to sit up.

"Hey, take it easy. You crashed in her yard. Some crazy old man ran you off the road. Do you remember?"

Allie squeezed her eyelids together, hoping it would make the pain go away. "I just heard a horn honking and then I crashed." She put her face in her hands and continued crying.

Paul drew her into his arms. "Ah, poor kid."

"What are *you* doing here?" she blubbered.

"I was on my way home from Jennifer Green's house. She only lives a block from here."

"Then you saw the whole thing."

"Well, kinda. I saw the car driving around the corner, but I didn't get a good look at what happened. I was worried about you, though—rippin' through Mrs. Hemmett's yard."

Allie giggled, then gingerly touched her face. "Ow, don't make me laugh."

Paul sat back. "Sorry. Yeah, you have a goose egg on the back of your head, and nasty scrapes on one side of your face and both hands." He gently dried some of her tears on his letterman's sweater.

"Ow!"

"Here, put this ice pack back on your face."

Allie took the ice bag, sighing as the cold hit her hands and face. "Did I faint?"

"You were knocked out cold."

"Really? Wow."

"Yeah, now you're just like a lot of the guys on the football team."

Allie looked around at her surroundings in a panic, waiting for Mrs. Hemmett's mangy old dog to slouch in and take a bite out of her leg. "What am I doing in this house?"

"Mrs. Hemmett heard the crash and found you in a heap in her yard. Then I came running, and she had me carry you in."

With this news came a fresh spate of tears. "I don't want to be here."

"I know. I called Dad. He should be here any minute."

"Where's Horrible Hemmett?" Allie whispered.

"She's making you some tea."

"Ugh! No. I'm not going to drink that." The tears turned into blubbering. "It's probably poisoned or something."

Paul patted her back. "It's okay. No worries. Dad will be here any second." He fished a roll of Life Savers out of his pocket. "Want one?"

Allie squinted at the offering. "I don't like wintergreen," she sobbed.

"Okay. Okay. Calm down. It's not the end of the world." He popped the piece of candy into his mouth and put the roll back into his pocket.

Mrs. Hemmett came out from the kitchen carrying a mug of tea and a couple of Oreo cookies.

Paul stood abruptly and swayed to one side. "Wow, sorry. I stood up too fast."

Mrs. Hemmett gave him a searching look. "Is that so?"

Paul steadied himself. "Maybe I'm not used to seeing my little sis in pain."

"Hmm." She held out the mug. "Does she want this?"

A car pulled into the driveway, and Paul took a deep breath. "I don't think so, Mrs. Hemmett, but thanks. That was very nice of you, but my dad's here now, and I'm sure he'll want to get her right home."

"Or to a doctor," Mrs. Hemmett said, setting the mug and cookies on the coffee table and moving to open the door.

"Yeah, maybe, but my mom's pretty great at patching things up."

Allie heard the door open and her dad's mumbled voice. "Let's go," she sniffed as Paul helped her up. "Get me out of here."

"You want me to carry you?"

"No. I can walk okay."

Her dad came into the room, and she greeted him with a new batch of tears. "Daddy, I fell off my bike."

He moved over to her, placing his hand tenderly on her back. "I know. I know. Not fun. Let's get you home and cleaned up. What do you say?"

Allie nodded and let the ice bag drop to the floor. She kept her head down as they moved past Mrs. Hemmett. "Sorry I crashed my bike in your yard."

"Wasn't your fault."

Allie glanced up, but Mrs. Hemmett wasn't looking at her. She was giving Paul an intense stare, which he avoided. Allie was in too much pain to think about it.

"Thanks, Mabel," Mr. Whitman said, as he took Allie's hand and helped her down the steps. "I'll be back tomorrow to pick up the bike."

"Your wife comes with the laundry tomorrow. She can get it then."

"That's right. I'll tell her. Thanks again."

There was no reply as the door snapped shut, and the rusted screen door screeched in the wind.

"Creepy," Paul said as he sprinted ahead to open the passenger-side door for Allie. He helped her get settled into the seat as their dad went around to the driver's side.

"Man, what's that smell?" Allie asked, weakly waving her scraped-up hand in front of her nose.

"Smell?" Paul said, taking a whiff of his letterman's sweater. "Ugh. Must be from Horrible Hemmett's house." He hopped into the back seat, rolled down the window, and stuck his head out.

"What are you doing? It's freezing out!" Allie scolded.

"I have to get rid of that smell!" Paul protested, popping another Life Saver into his mouth.

Mr. Whitman started the car. "Roll the window up, son. It's starting to rain."

Paul slowly did as he was told, but Allie heard him mumble, "I'd rather have the rain in my face than deal with that smell."

Allie started to giggle, but the pain in her cheek stopped her. "Ow." She closed her eyes and laid her head back against the seat. In her mind, she saw Horrible Hemmett's house with the green sofa and the braided area rug. She shuddered and was about to open her eyes when she remembered the rest of the room: no clutter, wood floor polished to a beautiful shine, and no dust on the coffee table. *Huh?* Allie opened her eyes and frowned. Mrs. Hemmett's house was cleaner than their own house. How was that possible? Her mom was a pretty good housekeeper, but usually there were magazines on the floor by the sofa, and dust on the side tables. *Was* Mrs. Hemmett a better housekeeper than her mom? Allie shook her head. The outside of Mrs. Hemmett's house had old peeling paint and a rusty screen door, but inside it was as neat as a pin and very clean. Allie was perplexed: If her house was that clean, then where was that strange smell coming from? Allie puzzled over it for a few seconds, then gave it up. As she looked down at her scraped and bloody hands, all she cared about was getting home and letting her mom take care of her. More tears rolled down her cheeks and Allie sniffed. Maybe, if she played her cards right, she could get some sympathy from her mom, and an extra serving of dessert after dinner.

Chapter Eight

"I have to go to school! Our science project is due today, and Frances is taking all the stuff. Her dad's driving her!"

Allie stood at the kitchen door in her pajamas as her mom cooked French toast, and Trudy sat at her corner table with her hands covering her face.

"Lower your voice," her mom said calmly, tapping Trudy lightly on the shoulder and holding out a graham cracker. Trudy kept one hand over her eyes and reached for the offering.

Paul looked up from pouring syrup on his stack of French toast. "You have the perfect excuse for a day off of school and you're not taking it?"

"Frances doesn't know about the crash. She'll expect me to be there."

Paul shrugged. "Well, with all your bandages, maybe the kids will think you're getting a head start on your mummy costume for Halloween."

"Paul, that's enough," her mom said, placing another plate of French toast on the lazy Susan. She gave Paul a stern look, but there was a slight smile at the corner of her mouth. "Stephanie, breakfast!" She pointed the spatula at Allie. "Sit and eat. I'll see what your dad says."

"Yes!" Allie said, raising one of her bandaged hands into the air. She slid into her chair and clumsily picked up her fork. Suddenly she was starving. Her bet was that her dad would let her go. She fished a piece of French toast onto her plate, then attempted a couple of sausages, which kept rolling off her fork. Just as their dad stepped into the kitchen, Paul grabbed two with his fingers and put them on Allie's plate.

"Forks are a wonderful invention, son."

"I don't care," Allie said quickly. "His hands are clean."

Her dad smiled and tapped her head with his morning newspaper. "Well, I wouldn't be too sure."

"Hey!" Paul said, a wounded tone in his voice. Allie giggled.

"How are you feeling this morning, young lady?"

"Good, Dad. Really good," Allie said, attempting to butter her French toast and failing. Paul came to her rescue again. "My hands hardly hurt at all."

"Well, they may not hurt, but they're not working very well. You sure you can navigate around school?"

Mom poured her dad a cup of coffee. "That's what I asked her, but she still wants to go."

He opened the paper to the headlines. "Maybe it would be better if you took the day off."

"No!" Allie said.

"No!" Trudy echoed from the corner. "Frances is taking all the stuff!"

Everyone looked over at Trudy as Stephanie came into the kitchen. "Frances is taking all what stuff?"

"The stuff for our science presentation. We have to turn it in today."

Stephanie gave Allie a wide-eyed stare. "And you still want to go to school looking like that?"

Mom set a bowl of fruit cocktail in front of her. "Stephanie."

"Sorry, Mom, but really, look at her. She should stay home."

"It's none of your business," Allie said, glaring at her.

"I had Mr. Nessen for a teacher. He's nice. He'd let you do your presentation at a different time."

Allie looked pleadingly at her dad. "But Frances is taking the stuff to school today!"

"Today! Today! Frances is taking the stuff today!" Trudy said loudly, banging her hand on her table. Mom went to quiet her.

"Okay, everyone just calm down," Dad said gently, lowering the paper. He turned to Paul. "Paul?"

Paul looked up in surprise, having just shoved a big piece of French toast into his mouth. "What?"

"You saw the crash, and you know about people being knocked unconscious because of your football buddies. I'm not really concerned about the scrapes, but I don't want to send her if there's any risk to her head."

"Too late for that," Stephanie said under her breath.

Paul swallowed and shrugged. "I don't know. She was only out a few minutes, but she had a little bit of a headache when she woke up."

"I don't have any headache now," Allie butted in.

"Let your brother finish."

"She wasn't seeing double or anything, and she didn't feel like puking. A lot of the guys puke when they've been knocked out."

"Gross," Stephanie said. "Do we have to have this conversation at the breakfast table?"

"Dad, I'm fine!" Allie said.

Her dad gave her a probing look. "No headache?"

"No."

"No seeing double?"

"No."

"No desire to puke?"

Allie giggled. "No."

He put two pieces of French toast and some sausages onto his plate. "Alright, you may go to school today."

"Yes!" Allie said, raising her bandaged hand into the air for a second time.

"But you go to the nurse's office immediately if you have any troubles. You hear me?"

"Yes, sir."

"They'll call us, and either your mother or I will come to pick you up." He went back to scanning the front page of the paper.

"Okay."

"Boy, you're a tough one, little sis," Paul said handing her another sausage. "That lady didn't know who she was dealing with."

"What lady?" Allie asked, biting into the sausage.

"The lady who honked you off the road."

Allie turned and frowned at him. "Lady? You said it was a little old man."

Paul's eyes flicked from Allie to their dad, who was looking over the top of the paper at him, and back again. "Really? Weird. It was pretty dark. Maybe it was a little old lady who looked like a little old man." Allie laughed. "I...I only saw the back of them when they went around the corner."

"Old people should not be allowed to drive," their mother said, sitting down at the table and putting a few sausages on her plate. "Just think. Allie's accident could have been much worse. Driving is a big responsibility."

"I agree, Patricia, there probably should be tougher tests for anyone over seventy."

"Probably? And I say it should start at sixty-five." She frowned over at Allie. "If you're going to school, little missy, you'd better not dawdle."

"Oh, yeah," Allie said, standing up.

"You don't need to go right this minute. Sit and finish your breakfast." She sat, and her mom poured her a glass of milk. "But you are definitely going to miss the bus."

"I'll drive her."

"Thanks, Dad!"

"Are you sure, Alan? With those hands it will take her a while to get dressed. I can drive her after I get Trudy ready."

"Nope, it'll be fine. I want to peek in and see her science project, anyway."

Allie choked on her sausage. "Ah, that's okay, Dad. You can just drop me off."

"But I'd like to see it."

"No, really."

"Why not? Did you end up making a volcano or something?"

"No, of course not. It's...it's just that everybody's gonna be staring at me, ya know? Because of this." She pointed to her bandaged face with her bandaged hand. "If you walk in with me, they'll think I'm a baby."

"You're not a baby," Trudy said.

"Thanks, Tru," Allie said, rolling her eyes. "Okay, Dad? Really, I'd just rather go in by myself."

"Okay, no need to get frantic. I'll boot you out at the curb. No problem." He smiled and went back to his reading.

Allie took a deep breath and shoved a piece of French toast into her mouth. "Thanks, Dad."

"Don't talk with your mouth full," her mom said as she moved to give Trudy another cracker.

Paul leaned over and whispered in Allie's ear, "Way to dodge a bullet, little sis."

Allie nodded several times, then pointed at him. "And you had better keep quiet."

"I'm as silent as Mr. Stubbs's grave."

"What are you two whispering about?" Stephanie asked.

Paul gave her a puzzled look. "We're sharing a secret, and it's none of your business. That's why we're whispering."

Dad's voice came from behind the paper. "It's not polite to whisper, son."

Allie gulped, but Paul took on the demeanor of repentance. "You're right, Dad. Sorry, Stephanie. We were talking about our Halloween costumes. Allie's going to be a mummy, of course, I'm going to be Zorro, and you're going to be the nosy neighbor in a hairnet and baggy bathrobe."

Allie burst out laughing.

"Dad," Stephanie whined.

"Paul, that was uncalled for, and Allie, stop laughing." Dad's voice was stern, but Allie noticed that he was having a hard time not laughing, too.

Just then came the honk of the school bus, and Stephanie jumped to her feet. "Oh, I have to get my coat." She hurried out of the kitchen.

Paul stood and went to get his gym bag. "Good luck on your science thing, Squirt!" He winked at her.

"Thanks, Paul."

Stephanie came back into the kitchen, grabbed her lunch, kissed her mom and dad on the cheek, and headed for the door.

"Tell Mr. Cross that Allie won't be on the bus today," Mom said.

"If I remember to."

"Stephanie."

"Okay, fine."

The back door closed, and her parents shared a look of amused aggravation, as Mrs. Whitman slid into her chair at the breakfast table. "Ah, two minutes of rest," she sighed, looking over at Allie. "If you're finished with your breakfast, go get ready."

Allie stood. "Okay." She fumbled with the plate and fork as she tried to clear her dishes.

"Never mind. I'll do it."

"Thanks, Mom!" She put down the fork and headed for the kitchen door.

"And I'll be in to do your hair in a few minutes."

"Great!"

As Allie laid out her plaid jumper dress and dark green turtle-neck, she kept thinking about how nice her mom was being. Was it because of her accident and her messed-up face and hands? Allie looked at the bandages on her hands and felt the skin twinge. Hmm... Even though it was painful, maybe she ought to crash her bike more often.

* * *

Allie watched Mr. Nessen with mingled anxiety and excitement as he walked slowly by the displays lining the perimeter of the classroom, awarding the grades for each science project. The students stood by their work, and Allie noticed that everyone looked nervous—everyone except Charlene Hastings and Ronald Miller. They were the smartest kids in the sixth grade so, of course, they knew they would get the highest mark. Their project had something to do with photosynthesis, and they had plants, and lights, and even a microscope that showed a thin slice of a leaf. It was cool, but Allie thought their dinosaur stuff was cooler.

Allie fidgeted as Mr. Nessen drew closer to their display. He only had four more grades to award. Todd Fisher and his partner got a rock symbol with a C in the center. They had done a volcano, and Allie thought they should have gotten a D. Their squatty mountain didn't even have lava spewing out, just a little smoke that lasted about five seconds. She wanted to catch Todd's eye, but he just kept looking at his shoes. Amanda Borden and Patty Flynn got a fish with a B for their project on geological samples. Now it was down to the eggheads and Frances and Allie. Ronald looked over at her and Frances, winking and giving them a crooked smile.

"He thinks they're going to get the top mark," Frances whispered to her. "Just 'cause his dad's a scientist."

Mr. Nessen stopped at the eggheads' display. "Well done, Charlene and Ronald. Well done." He shook their hands, then stuck a star with an A- in the center onto their board.

Allie stared as he came over to them and affixed a round yellow sun with a big red A in the center to her and Frances's dinosaur display board. He shook Frances's hand and patted Allie lightly on the shoulder.

"Well done, Frances and Allie. You have won the top mark among this year's science projects."

Frances squealed as the other class members clapped. "We did it!" she chirped in her high-pitched Frances voice. She started to grab Allie's hand, then remembered her injury, so instead she released her excitement by jumping up and down.

Allie was stunned. They had won the top mark! With her injuries, jumping wasn't an option, but her insides were doing their fair share of hopping up and down. "Thank you, Mr. Nessen! Thank you!"

"It is well deserved, girls. I definitely see the work involved." He winked at them. "Better than *Sputnik*." They nodded enthusiastically as he turned to another student.

A voice behind Allie said, "You guys did a great job."

Allie looked around to see Charlene Hastings standing in front of their display. "Ah...ah, thanks, Charlene."

"Where'd you get the skeleton?"

"I made it. Well, I mean, I didn't make it. I put it together. It was a dead pet I dug up and it was all bones, so I put it together." Allie knew she was babbling, but she couldn't help it. The smartest girl in sixth grade liked her dinosaur project!

"Keen," Charlene complimented. "I'm going to be a botanist, but maybe I'll minor in paleontology."

"Wow! That...that would be cool!" Allie stammered. She looked to see Frances's reaction and found her wide-eyed and gawking. "Frances, it's not polite to stare." Then she noticed that her friend wasn't staring at Charlene, but at something on the other side of the room.

"It's your mom!" Frances squeaked.

"What?" Allie leaned to the side and saw her mom standing at the door to the classroom and Mr. Nessen moving to greet her. "No! Oh, no!"

"And she has her camera," Frances informed Allie.

"She can't see Mr. Stubbs! She can't! She will be so mad at me. I'll be grounded forever!"

"What are we gonna do?"

"Hide him!"

"Where?"

"I don't care! Anywhere!"

Frances grabbed the small platform and turned in a few circles, searching for a hiding place.

"Go!" Allie hissed in desperation as she saw Mr. Nessen and her mom heading toward them.

Frances sprinted to Mr. Nessen's desk, pulled out his chair, set Mr. Stubbs on the seat, and shoved the chair back under the desktop. Several of the students were watching her with narrowed looks, so she smiled broadly and did her little Frances wave.

Allie was just about to pass out when the end-of-school bell rang, jolting her alert. She looked up into her mom's smiling face. "Mom! Hi! What are you doing here?"

"I came to pick you up."

"Oh, oh yeah."

Frances came, flustered, over to Allie's side. "Hi! Hi, Mrs. Whitman. What are you doing here?"

Mrs. Whitman gave Frances an amused look. "I'm here to pick Allie up from school."

"Oh, nice. Yeah, that's good 'cause of her hands and everything. Yeah, my dad's gonna come tomorrow to pick up all the stuff from our science project."

"For which you received the top mark, I understand."

"We did," Frances said, beaming.

At any other time, Allie would have cherished her mom's attention and warm smile, but her heart was still bumping against her ribs, and she felt like there was hot lava in her stomach.

"Allie, are you all right?" Mr. Nessen asked.

"What? Oh, yeah...yes! Yes, I'm fine. Just excited about our top mark."

"As you should be." He turned to Allie's mom. "It was evident they worked very hard, especially on the miniature—"

"So, Mom!" Allie interrupted. "Do you want to take a picture?"

"I do."

"Well, we better get going before Frances has to catch the bus."

Mr. Nessen smiled at them. "I'll leave you to it, then. Again, girls, job well done."

"Thank you, Mr. Nessen," they chorused.

As Mr. Nessen turned to encourage his other students to gather their belongings and exit the classroom, Mrs. Whitman readied Gertie to take the requisite pictures. "Okay, you two," she coached, "stand together holding that big dinosaur bone." They did as they were told, and Gertie captured several pictures of Frances smiling and Allie looking like she had hot lava in her stomach. The last picture was of Allie holding up the yellow sun with the A in the center. For this picture, she managed to force a slight smile at the corner of her mouth, even though she knew Gertie had captured a forever picture of her gauze-covered in-juries—and her deception. Her mother touched the sun as Allie pinned it back onto the board. "Your father will be pleased."

"Well, I have to get to the bus!" Frances said, grabbing her book bag and lunch box and edging toward the door.

"I'd offer to take you home, Frances, but we have to take the laundry and pick up Allie's bike at Mrs. Hemmett's."

"That's okay, Mrs. Whitman, I like the bus. See you tomorrow, Allie! Get better!"

"Thanks!" Allie said, moving over to pick up her backpack.

"I'll get that," her mom said. "Ready?"

"Yep, ah...yes, ma'am."

They were halfway down the hallway when Allie remembered that Mr. Stubbs was still sitting in Mr. Nessen's chair. She turned to run back.

"Allie?"

"I forgot my coat!"

"I can get it for you."

"No. That's okay. I'll do it." She raced into the classroom, pulled out Mr. Nessen's chair (which hurt her hands a lot), and fumbled to pick up the dino display. She winced as the board scraped against her injured hands. "Ow, ow, ow!"

"Miss Whitman?"

Allie almost dropped the board, as she watched Mr. Nessen come from the storage room. "Yikes! I mean, yes, Mr. Nessen?"

"What are you doing?"

"What am I doing with what? Oh, with this? Well, I...I..."

"Yes?"

"I was going to try and take it home to show my dad, but it's too hard to carry. Ya know, with my hands."

"I could carry it out for you."

"Oh, no, Mr. Nessen. Really. I'll just let Frances's dad get it tomorrow; then I can get it from her house."

"Are you sure? I wouldn't mind."

"No, I'm sure." She set the skeleton at their display and moved to get her coat. "That's very nice of you, but you've got other stuff to do. It's better if Frances and her dad pick it up."

"Whatever you think best," he said, smiling at her and moving to his desk. "It was very brave of you to come to school today, Miss Whitman."

Allie paused at the door. "Really?"

"Indeed."

"Thank you, Mr. Nessen."

"A person of less character might have used it as an excuse to miss school."

"Well, Frances was counting on me."

He gave her a warm smile. "As I said, well done."

As Allie went to meet her mom in the hallway, she wasn't thinking about how she had just dodged a very large bullet, or how she still had secrets to keep; she was thinking about other things she might do so that Mr. Nessen would say "well done" again. She felt so happy, she didn't even care that her mom was dragging her along to Horrible Hemmett's house. Well—she didn't care as long as her mom didn't make her carry one of the laundry baskets.

Chapter Nine

"**M**om, she's not home! Let's go!"
Mrs. Whitman rapped on the door for the fifth time. "She's always home."

"Well, not today. Let's go. My hands are really hurting."

"You were the one who wanted to go to school today."

The criticism in her mom's voice about her school choice was the opposite of Mr. Nessen's approval, and Allie turned abruptly from her mom's side to sit on the rickety steps. She placed her hands on her legs, palms up, and mumbled a string of peevish words to the universe.

"Don't mumble," her mother said, leaving the baskets sitting by the front door and moving past her down the stairs. She trekked around the side of the house.

"Where are you going?"

"To find Mrs. Hemmett."

Allie jumped up and ran after her. "Hey! Don't go back there!"

"For heaven's sake, why not?"

Cut-off animal heads! Allie thought, but what croaked from her mouth was, "Because it's trespassing!"

"It's not trespassing if you're legitimately looking for someone."

They reached the back of the house with its big backyard sloping down to pine and aspen trees at the edge of the meadow. You could see a section of the lake through the trees, and in the distance, Mr. Talac. *Man*, Allie thought, *some fancy family would pay a lot of money for this property.* She swallowed and looked around. *Until they found out it was haunted by a hundred headless animals.* "Mom, we really shouldn't be back here."

"Stop being a goose," her mother said, shading her eyes and squinting toward the edge of the meadow. She waved. "See! There she is, right there! Hi, Mabel!"

"Mom! Stop! Stop waving!" Allie hissed, for she had also spotted Horrible Hemmett lurking in the shadows. She was digging in what looked to be a miniature cemetery. Her mom started to walk down the hill. "Mom, she's burying something!"

"Don't be ridiculous. She's just working in her garden."

"In October?" Allie called out. She was torn between following her mom to the cemetery or staying alone by Horrible Hemmett's creepy house. She followed her mom.

"What's that sound?" Mrs. Whitman asked absently.

Probably the howling of a hundred animal ghosts, Allie surmised.

"Sounds like wind chimes or something." Her mom raised her hand again and called out. "Hello, Mrs. Hemmett! We didn't know where you were."

Mrs. Hemmett didn't answer, but just kept digging, and as they neared she stooped over and picked up something in a smudged pillowcase.

"Oh, my," Mrs. Whitman said when she realized they were indeed standing next to a small cemetery, complete with simple crosses and tombstones. Well, the tombstones were made of wood, but Allie had never heard anyone say "tomb woods." Her brain was short-circuiting with fear, and as she stood behind her mom, she felt a serious need to go to the bathroom. Allie shivered as Mrs. Hemmett gently laid the pillowcase in the grave and started shoveling dirt on top.

"Somebody hit a racoon. Just left it suffering by the side of the road."

"Oh? Oh dear. Oh, that's...well, that's terrible. A racoon?" Her mom was babbling, and even with all the shadow and scariness, Allie found it funny. She wanted to laugh, but she didn't—for many reasons. She peeked around her mom to get a better view of the creepy creature cemetery. There had to be twenty or thirty graves, each with its own cross or tombstone. Allie wondered how Mrs. Hemmett figured out which animals were Christians.

A chill wind blew against Allie's neck, and she heard again the fairy sound of tinkling glass and wind chimes. It was enchanting and seemed to bring swirls of magic into the gloaming. Allie peered into the dusk and discovered the small music makers tied to the arm of nearly every cross. Some were delicate tubes of metal hanging from Mason jar lids while others were pieces of multicolored glass attached with fishing line. With a shock, Allie realized that it must have been Mrs. Hemmett who had made them and then carefully tied them in place.

"How's your face?"

Allie jumped. "What?"

Mrs. Hemmett stopped shoveling dirt to look at her. "Your face. How are your face and hands feeling?"

"They hurt a little."

"Of course, you took quite a fall." She began shoveling again. "You two go up to the house, and I'll be right along."

Allie and her mom did as they were told.

As they walked up the slope, a hundred thoughts bumped around in Allie's head. Finally, one thought pushed its way to her mouth. "Why would people say she cut off the heads of animals and put them on poles?"

"Excuse me?"

"Poles. People in town say that she sticks animal heads on little poles."

"What people?"

"Mrs. Culp, your hairdresser, said she heard it from some people."

"Preposterous."

"What's that mean?"

"It means it's a stupid idea. Helen Culp has about as much sense as a porcupine."

Preposterous. Good word for her diary, Allie thought. "Yeah, but that's what some people say." They reached the top of the slope and stopped for a moment to catch their breath.

"You must not believe everything you hear, Allie."

"Even if it's a grown-up who says it?"

Her mom took a big breath (which usually meant she was tired of Allie's senseless questions) and turned to her. "Adults normally speak from knowledge and experience, and you must listen to what they say, but occasionally they get it wrong, or they exaggerate."

Which *means they tell big fat whoppers,* Allie thought. She didn't share that particular idea with her mom, of course. She just said, "Oh. Okay."

They moved around to stand on Mrs. Hemmett's front porch, and after a few minutes of cold wind and nervous waiting, Allie *really* needed to use the bathroom.

"Why are you wiggling around? Do you have to go to the bathroom?" her mother asked in an annoyed voice. Allie only had the chance to nod before the front door opened. "Oh, for heaven's sake," her mother said, looking at Mrs. Hemmett as she stepped forward. "I'm sorry, Mabel, but can Allie use your restroom?"

"Mom! It's okay!"

"It seems she didn't go before leaving school."

"Mom!"

"Sure," Mrs. Hemmett said, stepping aside and looking at Allie. "Down the hall, first door on the right."

"Really, I can wait."

Mrs. Hemmett smiled. "It's okay. I have toilet paper and everything."

"Huh?"

"Go on. First door on the right."

Another cold gust of wind and Allie's decision was made. "Okay. Thanks." She hurried past Mrs. Hemmett and straight to the hallway, hoping the mangy dog was just a figment of the townspeople's imaginations. As Allie relieved herself, she checked out the surroundings. Just like the rest of the house, the bathroom was spotlessly clean. Neither tub, sink, floor tiles, nor walls carried a speck of dirt or grime. There was a hand-braided rug on the floor, a painting of Mount Fuji on the wall, and the light smell of Clorox and lavender in the air. And just as Mrs. Hemmett promised, there was toilet paper. Allie came out of the bathroom and into the front room just as Mrs. Hemmett was setting down the second basket of laundry.

"Thank you, Mrs. Hemmett."

"No problem. You want a couple of Oreos?"

Allie loved Oreos. "Well, it's just before dinner, so I'd better not."

"Stick 'em in your pocket and eat 'em after."

"Allie? Are you finished?" her mom called from the porch. "I need to pick up Trudy at Miss Rose's house, then get home to fix dinner."

"See. I'd better go," Allie answered as she moved to the door.

"Okay, maybe next time," Mrs. Hemmett said following her out. "Let's go get your bike. It's over at the side of the house."

"Oh, that's right, the bike. I almost forgot," her mom said, following Mrs. Hemmett past the pile of flattened cardboard boxes. She brought her hands out of her pockets and picked up the bike. "My goodness, it's cold. Time to get out the gloves and scarves." She opened the trunk of the car, and with Mrs. Hemmett's help, maneuvered the bike inside.

"The lid's not gonna close," Allie pointed out.

"This is not news," her mom replied. "We only have a short way to go, and I'll drive slowly."

"Have you found out any more about who ran her off the road?" Mrs. Hemmett asked.

Mrs. Whitman shook her head. "No. Paul just says it was some older person. He can't remember the car color or anything. Of course, it was getting dark."

"Well, it wasn't *that* dark."

Allie thought that was a strange thing to say. Her mom must have thought so, too, because she stopped with her hand on the car door handle and gave Mrs. Hemmett a sideways look. "What do you mean, Mabel? Do you think Paul saw something he's not telling us?"

"That's your boy's story to tell." She turned back to her house. "See you Thursday for the laundry pickup."

"So very odd," her mom said as they got into the car. "Odd, odd, odd. I think that accident did more than disfigure her face."

Allie's head jerked around so fast, the scrape on her face blazed with pain. "Ow!" she croaked.

"What?" her mom asked, turning on the car and driving out of Mrs. Hemmett's yard. "Do you have something to say?"

Allie opened her mouth to say something, then closed it. She slowly shook her head. "Ah...no." She turned away from her mom to look out her window. If she had said anything so mean, she'd be grounded for a month. Allie felt queasy, and as they made their way home, her mom's words kept pecking at her brain. *Occasionally they get it wrong.*

Chapter Ten

Dad had built a fire, and for a few minutes, he and Allie were the only ones in the front room. Mom was putting Trudy to bed, and Paul and Stephanie were in their rooms studying. Allie was also doing homework, but she liked to work here, sitting in front of the fire in her pajamas, listening to the crackle of the burning logs, and having her dad help her.

"Ready for the next word?"

Allie sighed, took her eyes from the dancing flames, and smiled over at her spelling coach. "Ready."

"Cucumber."

"Cucumber. C U C U M B E R. Cucumber."

"Correct. Now, use it in a sentence."

"I ate a cucumber."

"Not very original."

Allie shrugged. "It's a good sentence."

Her dad raised his eyebrows. "Well, I'm not the one who wants to be a writer." As Allie started to protest, he quickly said, "Next word—consider."

"Consider. C O N S I D E R. Consider."

"Correct. Use it in a sentence."

"It was preposterous to consider that she would ever eat a cucumber."

Her dad laughed. "Smart-aleck. And *preposterous*—where'd you get that big word?"

"I'm not in fourth grade, ya know."

"This I do know—sixth grade, and winner of the top mark in science!"

"Dad."

"Well, that's what your mom said."

"I know, but don't make a big deal about it." She gave him a look that said, I'd rather not be bothered when actually it made her smile inside to have him mention it. She wondered if Charlene Hastings ever got tired of her parents talking about how smart she was.

Dad cleared his throat. "Pay attention, daydreamer. Last word. Committee."

Allie hesitated. "Ah...committee?"

Her dad nodded.

"Can we skip that one?"

"Will your teacher skip it on the test?"

"No."

"Okay, then. Committee."

"Committee. C O M I T T E. Committee."

"Incorrect."

Allie smacked her hand on the couch, then winced from the pain. *Well, so much for her delusions of smartness.* C O M...M I T E?

"Incorrect."

"Ugh!" Allie growled.

"Don't get upset. It's a tough one. Just think two m's, two t's, and two e's."

Allie sat up straighter. C O M M I T T E E?

"Correct!"

"Good thing that's the last word," Allie said, flopping back on the couch. "My brain feels like Cream of Wheat."

"Maybe you should head off for bed. It's been a busy day for you."

"Can I just lie here for a minute? The fire's nice."

"Well, maybe a minute. But don't go to sleep. You're too big to carry to bed anymore."

"I won't." Allie lay down on the couch and put a throw pillow under her head. Her dad put another log on the fire, then sat back in the recliner to read his *National Geographic*. Allie loved the bright yellow cover of the magazine and the picture of the

African savannah. She closed her eyes, and her thoughts drifted from elephants to the sun symbol with the big red A in its center, to the picture of Mount Fuji in Mrs. Hemmett's bathroom. The voices of her mom and dad whispered from within the bamboo forest at the foot of Mount Fuji. Allie pulled her brain from sleep to concentrate on what they were saying. It seemed to be some sort of argument, and Allie gave a little grunt and turned toward the back of the sofa to convince them she was asleep and not listening.

"Why did you let her fall asleep on the couch?"

"I told her not to."

"Well, that obviously didn't work, did it?"

Allie knew that her dad would use his typical "change the subject" tactic to avoid being scolded. "So, tell me why Mr. Rutherford called at this time of night..."

Why had Mr. Rutherford called? Allie wondered. He was the vice principal of the high school, an ex-marine and a no-nonsense kind of guy. Well, that's what she'd heard her dad say to Paul one day when her brother was complaining about Mr. Rutherford's tough rules.

"He said that Paul would not be playing in the next two football games because he's dropped below a C in two of his classes."

Allie's dad laid the magazine over on the side table. "When did this happen?"

"Obviously it's been going on for some time."

"Not to *our* knowledge."

"That's what I mean, Alan. He's struggling with his grades, and the first time the school decides to inform us is when he's banned from the team? That's pretty irresponsible. Paul hasn't mentioned anything to you about having trouble?"

"No. Not a word."

"I bet it's because of that time he was running around with that Mike kid."

Allie heard her dad stand. "Could be. I'll have a talk with him tomorrow."

"But, Alan..."

"Tomorrow, Patricia. I think it's time to get Allie to bed."

"We are not done talking about this," her mother stated flatly.

"I know, but right now, bed for Allie."

"What a nuisance," she heard her mother mumble. Allie cringed. Did her mother mean *she* was a nuisance or that her falling asleep in the front room was a nuisance?

"Hey, sleepyhead," her dad said as he gently nudged her. "Come on, now. I thought I told you not to go to sleep out here."

Allie groaned and pretended she was just waking up. "Huh?" she said drowsily.

"No sleeping, remember?"

"Sorry, Dad. The fire did it."

"Off to bed now," her mother interjected. "We'll have to do your bandages in the morning."

Allie stood and swayed a little. "Oh, okay. Thanks, Mom."

"I'll be waking you up earlier than usual so you can catch the bus."

Allie yawned. "That'll be good. Night." She moved past her dad. "Night, Dad." He patted her on the back, and she shuffled off to her room, going slowly up the stairs and making the most of her dramatic exit. Her mom and dad started talking again, but Allie couldn't make out the words. She sighed. She was too tired to think much about it, but as she passed Paul's room and saw light coming from under the door, she wondered what was going on with him. Her mom thought he wasn't going around with that Mike kid anymore, but Allie knew better. It wasn't like Paul to not do what he was told, or to get bad grades. Allie knew he wasn't as smart as Stephanie, but he always got by with Bs, and people really liked him. Mom often advised him that he was too charming for his own good, although she always said it with a smile at the corner of her mouth. The word *charming* made

Allie think of Prince Charming or of snake charmers in India, and neither one seemed authentic or good. *Authentic.* She liked that word. She'd written it in her diary during the summer after she'd seen a roadside stand with a banner that said, *Authentic California Artichokes.*

Allie stopped and laid her hand on Paul's door. "Paul?" she said softly. No sound came from his room. *Maybe he's fallen asleep early,* she thought. "Paul?" She tapped two times and heard his desk chair push back, and then footsteps. The door opened a crack, and Paul smiled at her.

"Hey, Squirt! What's up?"

Now that they were face-to-face, she didn't know what she wanted to say. "I...I was just going to bed."

He gave her a quizzical look, and then a wink. "Okay. Thanks for letting me know." He started to shut the door.

"Paul?" she said in a whisper.

"Yeah?" he whispered back with a grin.

"Well, I just thought you might want to know that Mom and Dad are downstairs talking about you."

The grin faded. "How do you know?"

"I pretended to be asleep on the couch."

Now, the charming Paul face was completely gone. "What were they saying?"

"Mr. Rutherford called from the school, and..."

Paul swore.

"Paul!"

"Did you hear what he told them?"

Allie was sorry she'd stopped at his door. She could be in her bed right now drifting off to dream land.

"Allie?"

"He told them you wouldn't be playing football for a while."

Paul swore again.

Allie flinched at the bad word. "Maybe I shouldn't have told you, but Dad said he was going to talk to you tomorrow, so I thought you might want to know."

"What? Oh, yeah. No, that's good, Squirt. Thanks. Now I have time to get my story together."

Allie felt he was talking more to himself than to her. "What story?"

Paul looked down at her, attempting a charming "Paul" smile that fell flat. "Nothing to worry about," he said, ruffling her hair. "You'd better get to bed now."

"Okay." She stepped back from him, smoothing her hair. "Are you in big trouble?"

"Nah. This will blow over. Dad and I'll talk it out. You know Dad. Thanks again for the heads-up."

"Sure."

He looked her straight in the eyes. "And, we're still partners in crime, right? You keep my secret and I'll keep yours?"

He'd asked it like a question, but it sounded more like a command. It was like when her mom said, "*You're going to mind your manners, right?*" when she really meant, *mind your manners or else*. Allie blinked. "Yeah, sure. Of course. Partners in crime."

Paul nodded and shut the door. Allie heard another swear word from the other side as she turned toward her room. She'd never heard that many bad words come from Paul's mouth. Well, except for the time when he broke his arm sledding, and then it was one bad word that rhymed with ham, said over and over again, until Mom gently put a stick into his mouth and made him bite on it.

Allie brushed her teeth, climbed into bed, and pulled the quilt up to her chin. Her stomach felt angry like it was having a hard time digesting the final dumpling she'd eaten from her mom's chicken and dumpling dinner. She heard the wind moaning in the pines and turned her head to look out the bedroom window. *Was there a snowstorm coming?* She hoped not. She loved snow for Thanksgiving and Christmas, but it was dreadful for Halloween. Just another thing to worry about—snow, secrets, homework, Halloween costumes, and now having a new Paul bumping around in the house. She groaned and turned onto her side. She liked the old Paul better.

Chapter Eleven

The next morning was dreadful.

Mom scorched the oatmeal because Trudy had thrown up on the kitchen floor and she was mopping up and not paying attention. Trudy threw up because she could hear Paul and Dad's raised voices from Dad's office. Mom yelled at Stephanie for letting the oatmeal burn, and Stephanie yelled at Allie because she'd run from the room at the first sign of vomit. And Allie almost missed the bus because Mom hadn't had time to change her bandages and she had to do it herself. Subsequently, she had tendrils of gauze hanging from her hands. She thought that maybe she *should* be a mummy for Halloween because she was looking more like one every day. Allie glanced at her terrible nursing job, dragged herself to the seat in the bus next to Frances, and plopped down.

"Wow! You look terrible," Frances observed.

"Thanks a lot," Allie mumbled.

Frances pulled a comb from her bag and started combing Allie's hair. "I'll help."

"Thanks."

Stephanie walked down the bus aisle with a scowl on her face. She dropped Allie's lunch box into her lap as she passed. "You forgot this."

"Ow!" Allie protested as the box landed on her bandaged hands.

"What happened at *your* house this morning?" Frances asked, warily watching Stephanie out of the corner of her eye as she tramped to the back of the bus.

"World War Two."

"How come?"

"Paul and Dad got into an argument."

"*Your* dad was arguing? About what?"

"Paul's grades. A couple of his classes are heading down the drain, and now he can't play football for a while."

"That's not so bad, is it?"

"At our house, it's bad. And then Trudy threw up..."

"Ewww," Frances said, making a sick Frances face. "Don't tell me anything about throw-up. I'll start gagging any second!"

"Okay. Okay. I don't need a repeat performance," Allie said. "Let's talk about something else."

"Oh! Oh! Oh!" Frances said, bouncing in her seat. "I have something great to tell you!"

"What? And please stop bouncing. It hurts my hands."

Frances stopped immediately. "Sorry. I'm just so excited."

"So, what is it?"

"Do you have your Halloween costume yet?"

Allie took a deep breath and tried not to be peeved. She was sure Frances was going to tell her about some fabulous Dorothy-from-the-Wizard-of-Oz costume that her mother had magically whipped up for her. "No," Allie said, holding up her hands. "I might just have to go as a half-done mummy."

"Or...you could be my twin!" Frances said with a squeal.

Allie looked at Frances's bushy dark hair and brown eyes and compared it to her own mousy brown hair and blue eyes, then said, "Huh?"

Frances laughed. "Not my *twin* twin. My mom was shopping in Reno yesterday, and she found this darling costume, so she picked up two! One for me and one for you!"

"Really? What is it?"

"Chickens!"

"Chickens?"

"Well, not chickens, but baby chicks coming out of their eggs! They are so cute! There's the egg and it's cracked, that's what you wear on the bottom—it comes up to about here." Frances motioned to chest high, and when Allie didn't respond, she burbled on with the description. "Then the top part is you as the baby chick with bright yellow wings and a feather cap you put on your head. Oh! And on the cap is this piece of broken eggshell. It's so cute!"

Allie was thinking of other C words, like *corny* or *childish*, but since Frances was so excited about it, she kept her mouth shut.

"And we won't need to worry if it's cold, because we can wear yellow tights and our heavy yellow sweaters, and we'll be fine!"

"I don't have yellow tights or a yellow sweater," Allie said distractedly, her brain still trying to conjure up the picture of a cracked egg and a yellow feather cap on top of her head.

"I have extras!"

"Huh?"

"I have extra yellow tights!"

"You do?"

"And you could wear a white sweater."

"I guess so."

Frances frowned. "You don't want to be a baby chick, do you?"

"I didn't say that."

"Well, you're not excited or anything," Frances said, sitting back in the seat and crossing her arms.

"No...it's just that...I'm kind of thinking of other things this morning."

"World War Two," Frances said glumly.

"Exactly. But I think the costume will be great."

"Really?"

"Really. Baby chicks popping out of their eggs? Really funny."

Frances grinned and sat forward. "I think so, too! No one will have a costume like us."

"That's for sure," Allie mumbled.

"What'd you say?" Frances asked, still grinning.

Allie turned to her friend. "I said it was nice—sure nice of your mom to think of me."

"Well, we're best friends," Frances said, giving her a quick hug. "And I think we're going to win the prize for best costume, don't you?"

"That would be cool," Allie said with forced enthusiasm—now dreading the school Halloween party. She imagined her classmates laughing and pointing at her and Frances as they imitated a hen laying an egg. Allie sighed and turned to look out the window across the aisle.

They were stopped at the intersection of Los Angeles Boulevard and Highway 50, and Mr. Cross was whistling a little tune and waiting for a break in the traffic, so he could pull out onto the main road. The bus started forward when suddenly Mr. Cross slammed on the brakes, jolting kids out of their seats. Allie instinctively thrust out her hands to push off from the seat in front of her, and pain shot from her hands up into her arms. Frances flew forward and clonked her head on the seat, then landed on the floor. She immediately started crying. There were shouts and cries all around the bus as Mr. Cross laid on the horn. "Stupid punk," he yelled. Allie had a quick glimpse of a blue and white sedan as it swerved around the bus and took off down Highway 50 toward the state line.

Mr. Cross threw open his side window and shouted at the departing car, "I'm calling the cops, you stupid punk!"

Allie was shaken up, not only from the abrupt stop, but by Mr. Cross's scary temper. She had never seen him angry before: Kids hollering, kids getting into fights, kids sticking their heads out the bus window—none of that had made him shout. He'd calmly pull the bus to the side of the road and walk back to take care of the situation. Just his standing up would always make the bus go quiet. Of course, he was a giant person, someone who could probably grind your bones to make his bread, so even the toughest kids didn't challenge him.

As he was pulling the bus to the side of the road, Stephanie came down the aisle to their seat. "Are you guys okay?"

Frances was still whimpering and rubbing her head.

"My hands hurt and Frances whacked her head, but I think we're okay. Frances?"

"Huh?"

"Are you okay?"

"I guess so. My head hurts. What happened?"

"A car pulled right in front of the bus," Stephanie said.

"Yeah, I know that car," Allie grumbled.

"What do you mean?" Stephanie snapped. "How do you know that car?"

Allie tried to mask the shocked look on her face, but it was too late. Her stumbling words didn't make for an effective denial, either. "I...I just mean that I've seen it around...on the streets. Just around on the streets. You've seen it, too, right?"

Stephanie frowned at her. "That's not what you said, little sis. Come on; spill it."

Allie was saved the telling, because Mr. Cross was marching down the aisle, checking on kids, and giving instructions. "Okay, everybody back in their seats. If you have an injury of any kind, raise your hand." The hands of about half the kids on the bus went up, and Mr. Cross growled. "Okay. When we get to the school, I want those with injuries to report immediately to the nurse." He pulled out his handkerchief and handed it to Todd Fisher, whose nose was bleeding. "Okay, everybody calm down. We'll get this sorted out." He went back to the driver's seat, started the engine, and slowly pulled out onto the road. Allie guessed he figured none of the kids were seriously injured because nobody was passed out or hollering in pain.

When they arrived at school, Allie and Frances took off at a fast walk for the middle school nurse. Stephanie called after her, but Allie pretended not to hear.

"Hey! Your sister wants to talk to you."

"Don't look around—just keep walking. We have to get to the nurse before the crowd arrives, and besides, I don't want to talk to her."

"Why not?"

"Because she's just gonna ask me about how come I know that Mike kid's car, and then somehow she'll wheedle it out of me that Paul is still riding around with him even though Mom's told him not to, and then...oh, never mind. It would just be a big mess."

"Yeah, it's already making my head hurt."

"Okay, then let's forget about it."

Allie took a deep breath as they moved into the school. She knew her sister wouldn't forget about it, and she knew she couldn't keep avoiding her forever. She'd just have to come up with some story so she could keep Paul's secret, and he could keep hers.

There were only two people in front of them as they lined up for the nurse—Todd Fisher with his bloody nose, and Charlene Hastings with a purplish splotch on her forehead. Allie looked around to find Mr. Cross escorting a few middle school kids toward the office. He looked like he wanted to punch somebody. Wow! Allie thought. *That Mike kid doesn't know what's coming his way.*

Chapter Twelve

"*Quack, quack, quack,*" Allie said as she marched around Frances's bedroom in her chick costume.

Frances fell onto her bed, laughing. "That's a duck sound, you doofus. Chicks go *peep, peep, peep.*"

"Well, maybe I'm a baby duck."

"You can't be a baby duck because I'm a baby chick and we're twins, remember?"

"*Peep, peep, peep,*" Allie chirped as she stopped at the mirror to look at her yellow sweater and fluffy yellow wings. *Pretty cute,* she thought. Her mom had taken one of her old white sweaters and dumped it in yellow Ritz dye, which had mostly worked. There were only a few splotches at the back, and those were covered by the costume. Allie flapped her fluffy yellow wings and admired her feather cap. It made her round face seem slimmer. She was feeling more confident about the school Halloween party.

Mrs. Catera stepped to the doorway of Frances's room "Oh, girls, you look adorable," she cooed. "Absolutely adorable! But now it's time to take off your costumes so you don't muss them before tomorrow."

"Ahhh," Frances moaned.

"Do not talk back, young lady. Besides, it's time for Allie to run home to dinner."

"You're right, Mrs. Catera," Allie said sliding the suspenders off her shoulders and stepping out of the half-cracked eggshell. "This really is a great costume. Thanks a ton for getting it for me!"

Mrs. Catera winced at Allie's use of slang, then she composed her face and smiled. "You are very welcome, Allie." She began to help Frances remove her costume. "I realize with everything your mother has on her plate; she doesn't have much time for such things as Halloween costumes and PTA bake sales."

"Huh?" Allie questioned as she removed her feather cap.

"Oh, it's nothing. Never you mind. Your mother does the best she can," Mrs. Catera said in a light tone. "Here, hand me your costume and I'll hang them up. Then they'll be nice and crisp for tomorrow." She turned in the doorway. "You are coming here to get dressed in the morning, correct?"

"That's the plan," Frances said. "Right, Allie?"

Allie nodded.

"Fine. Then I will drive you to school so there's no risk of getting grime on them from the school bus."

"Good idea, Mom."

"Allie, are you alright?" Mrs. Catera asked.

Allie jumped. "Me?"

"Yes. You look like you're a hundred miles away."

Allie put on a fake smile. "Oh, no. It's nothing. I...I was just thinking about tomorrow. I hope it doesn't snow or anything."

"The weatherman said no rain or snow," Mrs. Catera assured as she moved into the hallway.

"That's a relief," Allie mumbled as she put on her skirt.

Frances frowned at her. "What's wrong with you?"

"Nothing!" Allie snapped. "Why does everyone keep asking me what's wrong with me. Nothing is wrong! Okay?"

"Holy smokes! Okay. Don't bite my head off."

Allie picked up her book bag. "Sorry. I'd better be getting home."

"I'll walk you downstairs."

"No, that's okay."

"Hey, what is wrong? All of a sudden you're all grumpy."

"It's nothing." Allie moved to the door, but Frances blocked her way.

"Oscar Meyer Bologna."

"It's nothing—I just wondered what your mom was saying about the PTA bake sale."

"The what?"

"The bake sale. Your mom said my mom didn't have time for Halloween costumes and the PTA bake sale."

Frances shrugged. "I don't know. My mom was in charge of it last week. It was to get money for new encyclopedias for the school library. Maybe your mom couldn't bake anything."

"My mom can bake stuff."

"I didn't mean that. Maybe she just didn't have time."

Allie felt tears press at the back of her eyes. "Well, maybe my mom was too busy for a stupid bake sale!"

"Hey! It wasn't stupid! My mom worked hard on it."

"It's stupid if I say it's stupid!"

Frances clenched her fists. "You're stupid!

"Just cause your mom only has one stupid kid, so she has time for stupid bake sales!"

Mrs. Catera came quickly into the room. "Girls! What in the world is all this shouting about?"

Frances stood dumbfounded, staring at Allie, and unable to answer her mother's question.

Allie felt her face go hot with shame. She shouldn't have said that thing about Frances's family having one stupid kid. She knew Frances's dream was to have a bunch of sisters and brothers. "I...I gotta get home," Allie stammered. "See you in the morning." She bolted for the door.

"No." Frances said hotly. "Take your costume with you."

Allie stopped dead in her tracks.

"Frances Elizabeth Catera! That is no way to speak to your friend."

"She's not my friend."

"Frances!"

"No, I mean it." She ran out of her bedroom, and Allie heard the bathroom door slam.

Mrs. Catera frowned at Allie then left the room.

Allie swallowed her tears, hefted her book bag, and headed for the door. Mrs. Catera met her at the top of the stairs with her costume. She held it out to her with the same frown. Allie took the cracked egg and bit her bottom lip. She wanted to say something, but all her words were stuck to the roof of her mouth like peanut butter. She turned and started down the stairs.

"Ungrateful," Mrs. Catera said.

Tears popped from Allie's eyes, making it difficult to navigate the last few steps and to see the doorknob. Her book bag and costume got tangled when she tried to turn the knob, and she growled in frustration and sadness. The door finally opened, and Allie stumbled out into the cold afternoon air. She'd forgotten to put on her coat, but she wasn't going back for it. She wiped her face with the sleeve of her yellow sweater, swung the costume over her shoulder, and lifted her book bag. *Stupid Mrs. Catera. Stupid bake sale. Stupid chicken costume!*

Chapter Thirteen

The next morning, Allie put on her chick costume without any joy. *Disheartened*, she thought. *That's what I am. Disheartened.* She'd found the word and the definition in the back of her diary the night before, and it seemed to fit her feelings perfectly. She sighed as she looked in the mirror. She didn't even want to go to school or wear this stupid costume, but she'd be even more disheartened if she missed the Halloween party, and she couldn't show up in her regular school clothes, 'cause then she'd look really dumb. Allie sighed again, deciding that she would spend the day with Sharon Smith, giggling and talking about boys.

As she trudged down the hallway, she heard Stephanie and Paul's voices coming from Paul's bedroom. She stopped and put her ear to the door.

"So, where were you that night?"

"At Jennifer Green's hou..."

"No, you weren't."

"What do you mean?"

"You weren't at Jennifer Green's. She told me you've never been to her house."

"What's this third degree? And why are you talking to Jennifer?"

"She and I were discussing the science club, but that's not the point."

"It *is* the point if you're nosing into my business."

Allie bit her bottom lip. They were both speaking in hushed voices, but Paul's voice sounded scary-mean.

"I'm not nosing into your business."

"Yeah, you are. Talking to Jennifer behind my back?"

Stephanie persisted. "Paul, you told Dad and Mom that you were at Jennifer's that night Allie crashed her bike, but you weren't."

Allie's insides jumped.

"Like I said, bug off!"

"And now your grades are dropping?"

"Stay out of my—"

Stephanie interrupted. "Oh, no. This is my business. I've taken extra time to help you with your homework, and now you're getting Ds in two of your classes?"

Paul swore. "Get off my back, Steph! First Mom and Dad, and now you? I don't need this third degree. Get out of my room."

Allie heard footsteps nearing the door. She panicked and knocked. The door flew open, and Paul glared down at her.

"What do *you* want?"

"Oh! Wow! Both you and Stephanie are here. I didn't know that. I mean, good...good, 'cause I wanted to show you guys my costume." She flapped her arms. "What do you think?"

"Cute," Stephanie said flatly as she pushed her way past Paul and hurried down the stairs.

"Yeah, cute," Paul said. He shut the door in her face.

Allie made her way to the kitchen, where even the smell of frying sausages couldn't make her smile. She frowned at her sister Trudy, who was wearing a paper plate hat with cotton balls stuck on the top. "What's she got on her head?"

"She's a cloud," Mrs. Whitman said, scooping eggs onto a plate.

Trudy glanced over at Allie as she maneuvered her way into her chair. "And we're having you for breakfast," she announced.

Allie groaned. "Wow, very funny."

"That was funny, Tru," Mrs. Whitman said, handing Trudy a graham cracker, then placing a plate of scrambled eggs and sausage in front of Allie. "And now we have an egg eating an egg."

"An egg eating an egg. An egg eating an egg," Trudy repeated.

"You two are hilarious," Allie grumbled. "Funnier than Abbott and Costello."

"Somebody sounds like a rotten egg this morning," her mom said as she headed back to the stove.

Allie jabbed her fork into a sausage. "Mom, really. I just have a lot on my mind."

"Ah, poor little egghead," her mom said with a chuckle.

Allie groaned and started eating. *You could say something nice about my costume,* she thought disappointedly.

"Where's Dad?" Stephanie asked as she stomped into the kitchen, throwing her book bag onto the floor. The sharp sound made Trudy jump and cover her ears.

"Too loud! Too loud!" she yelped, ripping the cloud hat off her head.

"Stephanie May Whitman! What is wrong with you?" Mrs. Whitman said in a falsely controlled voice. She went over and knelt by Trudy's side, drumming her fingers on the table to distract her rocking.

Stephanie took a deep breath. "Sorry." She took a step toward her sister. "Sorry, Tru."

"Too loud. You are too loud."

"I know, Tru. I'm sorry. I promise to be quiet." Stephanie sat down and poured herself a glass of apple juice. "So, where is he?"

"He had an early client. Why do you need him?"

"I just need to talk to him about some school stuff."

Mom stood and went to crack four eggs into the frying pan. "School stuff you can't discuss with me?"

Stephanie slowly spooned fruit cocktail into her bowl. "Ah, well...it just concerns fund-raising for the science club. I was going to ask him if his office wanted to contribute."

Boy! Allie thought. *This family is really great at telling whoppers.*

"Oh, is that all? Well, you can ask him tonight."

"Not tonight!" Allie blurted.

"Why not?" Mom and Stephanie said together.

"Because he has to take me trick-or-treating."

Mom flipped the eggs and turned to look at her. "I thought Frances's dad was taking you."

"He can't. He has...something else to do."

Her mom stepped to the kitchen door. "Paul, breakfast in one minute!" She went back to the stove, mumbling to herself although everyone could hear. "People think they're the only ones with something to do." She shook her head. "I suppose Frances will need a ride, then?"

"No. No, she's going with someone else."

Her mom slid the eggs onto a plate. "Someone else?" She put toast and sausage next to the eggs and set the plate on the table. "But I thought you two had twin costumes."

Luckily Paul came into the kitchen at that moment. He slung his gym bag over his shoulder, grabbed his fork, and reached down to scoop the eggs and sausage onto one piece of toast, then smash the other piece on top.

Mom stared at him. "Paul, you're making a mess! Sit down and eat."

"Can't. Gotta be at school early."

"Meeting Jennifer Green?" Stephanie asked in her most obnoxious voice.

"Shut up!" Paul said in his most threatening voice.

"Paul Alan Whitman!" Mom said in her most shocked voice.

Paul went out the back door without another word, slamming the door and leaving everyone in a moment of stunned silence.

"What is wrong with this family lately?" Mom said as she went to turn off the stove.

"Paul's what's wrong," Stephanie said, an uncharacteristic tremor of tears in her voice.

Allie stiffened, waiting for the truth about Paul to spill out of Stephanie's mouth.

"Oh, Stephanie, don't be so dramatic." Mom said, pouring herself a cup of coffee and grabbing her English muffin. "He's just upset about not being able to play football for a while."

Allie stared at her mom as though she had a monkey on her head.

Stephanie growled. "Why do you always do that? Why do you always take his side?"

"Watch your tone, young lady," Mom returned tersely. "And I do not always take his side."

"Yes, you do. Or at least you minimize his bad behavior."

Allie turned to stare at her sister. *That's exactly what Mom did*, Allie thought. *Stephanie had it just right. Paul is the third favorite after Trudy and Dad, and Mom gives him a lot of passes on his behavior.*

"He's grounded until his grades are up. That's certainly not minimizing," Mom said in an even tone.

The bus horn sounded.

Stephanie growled again. "Right. If you only knew." She picked up her bag and slogged out the door.

"And what do you mean by that?" Mom snapped, but Stephanie was gone.

Allie wobbled onto her feet, grabbed her lunch box and school bag, and headed off.

"No 'thank you for breakfast'?" her mom's voice called after her.

"Thanks for breakfast!"

Her mom said something else, but Allie couldn't make it out. She was too busy holding on to all her stuff and keeping her suspenders on her shoulders.

As she waddled to the bus, she hoped Mr. Cross would take pity on a little cracked chicken and give her a few extra minutes today.

Chapter Fourteen

She sat alone on the bus, because, of course, Frances's mother had driven the other egg to school so her costume wouldn't get grimy. Allie sighed and looked down at her hands. They were mostly healed up now, as was the scrape on her face. She sighed again. She saw herself going from one catastrophe to another, and she remembered clearly when she'd written "*catastrophe*" in the back of her diary. It was two months ago, the first day of sixth grade, when a robin pooped on her shoulder as she got off the bus. Catastrophe! Even Frances laughed at her for a second before grabbing her hand and racing with her to the bathroom.

She missed Frances. By now, if they hadn't had the fight, they'd be making up a secret chicken language sort of like Pig Latin, but cuter, and they'd be telling chicken jokes.

Why was the baby chicken a chicken?

Because it was yellow.

The bus pulled up to the curb at South Tahoe High School and the students piled out. Allie waited until last, so she wouldn't have a bunch of kids surrounding her and making wisecracks. Even though the wing for the middle grades was apart from the high school, sometimes the front entrance was a jumble of ages until they separated for their individual territories.

Mr. Cross was writing on his clipboard as she passed. He didn't look up, but his low, rumbly voice followed her.

"I must say, Miss Allie, one of the best costumes I've ever seen."

She stopped and turned back. "Really?"

"Yes, indeed."

"Thank you, Mr. Cross."

"You're welcome."

She got off the bus, wanting to skip all the way to the entrance; she didn't, of course, because skipping was so fourth grade, but she was happy that she felt like it. When she got into her classroom she avoided looking at Frances, who was helping Mr. Nessen place some sort of school pamphlet on the desks. Instead, she searched for Sharon. She was at the back of the room, by the cupboard, playing rock, paper, scissors with two boys.

This is going to be awkward, Allie thought as she moved to put her lunch box and book bag in her cupboard spot. Especially awkward because Sharon's costume was darling and sophisticated. She was an Egyptian princess, complete with a dark black wig dripping with jewels. Allie suddenly felt very yellow and very second grade. Maybe it would be better to just hang out by herself today.

She shoved her lunch box into its slot, took her books out of her bag, and hung the bag on the hook. She jumped as she closed the door to the cupboard when she found Sharon standing on the other side.

"I might have known you and Frances would come as twins," Sharon said.

Allie glanced over at Frances. They made eye contact for a moment, then Frances flipped her fluffy little egg head in the opposite direction.

"Yeah, well, she's mad at me right now."

"Really?" Sharon said, a note of excitement in her voice. "How come?"

"Oh, it's a long story," Allie said with a shrug. She moved to her desk to put her books away, and Sharon lifted the desktop for her.

"So, you're not going to walk together in the parade?"

"Probably not."

Sharon brightened. "We could walk together!"

"That'd be great," Allie answered, trying to sound nonchalant.

"Your costume is darling," Sharon said. "And you look much cuter than Frances."

"Thanks," Allie answered, wondering how her costume could look cuter when they were exactly the same.

The bell rang.

"Your costume is beautiful," Allie whispered as Sharon headed off to her desk.

Sharon smiled. "Thanks."

As the class went over the pamphlet on proper dental hygiene, Allie's mind wandered back to third, fourth, and fifth grade, when she, Sharon, and Frances had been "The Three Musketeers"— they had done everything together: homework, bike riding, sleepovers, walks to the meadow, picnics at the beach, swimming lessons, Girl Scouts—sometimes they even shared their chores. They were pals forever, until this past summer, when Sharon went with her family to Europe for two months so her father could work on some economic council in Germany. She came home saying things in German—like *loffel* for spoon and *katze* for cat. It was irritating. It was also irritating how often she chose to ditch them and spend time with the neighborhood boys, or how many times she told them that the things they used to do together were boring and childish. Finally, Allie and Frances stopped calling her with all their boring and childish ideas, and the Three Musketeers disbanded.

Allie turned in her seat to look at Sharon, who smiled and waved. Hmm...maybe it wouldn't be so bad to hang out with Cleopatra and talk about boys, although Allie figured her side of the conversation would be short, as what she knew about boys would fit in a thimble.

* * *

The rest of the day went better than Allie had expected. She and Sharon ate lunch together, and "the twins" joined them. Jimmy and John Backman were popular seventh graders and played some new European sport called soccer. They were dressed in their soccer shirts, with their hair all messed up like they'd just finished a game. They looked cool, and Allie kept glancing over to see their grins and watch them put food into their mouths. They liked talking to Sharon, because she laughed at their stupid jokes and she knew something about soccer, having lived in Germany. Allie did her best to laugh at the jokes and nod her head when John talked about different European soccer teams, but in truth, she got kind of tired of "boy talk" after about fifteen minutes. She also got tired of Jimmy Backman patting her head and saying, "Poor little Humpty Dumpty." Despite all that, it felt very grown-up to be sitting next to boys. Allie only wished that she was wearing a twin Egyptian princess costume like Sharon instead of Frances's Chicken Little getup.

At the costume parade, she and Sharon got a lot of attention—well, mostly Sharon, but since Allie was right next to her, she pretended the applause was for her. Jimmy Backman even winked at her at one point, which caused her to flap her wings. She felt really dumb afterward, but Sharon just laughed and teased her about having a crush on Jimmy Backman. No such thing; he just made her nervous.

Allie stopped smiling when she noticed Frances walking by herself. Her friend had been so excited about the chicken costumes, and now she looked like all she wanted to do was go home. Allie was thinking about catching up to her and walking the last part of the parade together, but she was afraid Frances would just tell her to "get lost" or that Sharon would feel abandoned.

The school day ended with cupcakes from the PTA, and Sharon winning a prize for most beautiful costume. Charlene Hastings won for most creative. She was a tropical rain forest with fake plants and flowers sewn all over a green pair of pants and turtleneck. Allie didn't understand it, but obviously the teachers thought it was brilliant. And, surprise of all surprises, she and Frances won the prize together for cutest costume. It was awkward standing next to Frances as they selected their candy bars, but at least Frances smiled over at her, which made Allie think they might be friends again.

"Hey! Congratulations!" Sharon said as she came over to them, holding up her own candy prize.

"You, too!" Allie said.

"Yeah, your costume is so exotic," Frances added.

"Exotic," Allie said, looking impressed. "Good word!"

"Well, I'm not in fourth grade," Frances said indignantly, and the three friends laughed together. Sharon turned to talk to Todd Fisher, who was dressed as a ghost with a white face and red blood dripping from the corner of his mouth. Allie wondered where the blood came from, since technically ghosts didn't have blood.

Frances cleared her throat. "So...ah..."

Allie took over. "I...I'm sorry I got mad yesterday."

"Me too," Frances admitted. She stood straighter. "But my mom's bake sale wasn't stupid."

"And my mom isn't a bad mom just because she didn't bake anything."

"Nobody said she was a bad mom. It's just that she's really busy."

"Well, she *is* busy!" Allie blurted out.

"I know!" Frances said, taking a deep breath. "That's what I said."

It was good that all the other kids were talking, laughing, and messing around because it masked the girls' quarrel.

"Okay, okay! Sorry." Allie said. "I don't want to get into this fight all over again."

"Me, either."

"I don't know what got into me yesterday," Allie admitted.

"Me, either," Frances said. "Wait! Wait! I don't mean you! I meant me! I don't know what got into *me*."

Allie nodded. "Yeah, I understand."

"It's been a crummy day," Frances continued.

It had been an okay day for Allie, but she wasn't going to say that. "Yeah, a crummy day."

Frances smiled. "Except that we won for cutest costume!"

"We did!" Allie said, flapping her wings and turning in a circle. "Your mom's gonna be so excited."

"I know, because we're so adorable," Frances said, mimicking her mom.

Allie and Frances laughed.

Sharon turned back to them. "Hey! Are you guys over being mad at each other?"

"I think so," Allie said.

Sharon smiled. "Good. Then I think we should all go out trick-or-treating together. What do you say?"

"Yeah!" Frances said quickly.

"That'd be great," Allie said.

"The Three Musketeers back together again!" Sharon said, holding up her candy bar like a sword.

The other two held up their candy bars, as well. "All for one and one for all!"

The bell rang, and Allie went to her desk to get her math book. She watched as Frances and Sharon walked to the cupboards together, chattering away as though there'd never been a separation. Allie smiled. She couldn't wait for trick-or-treating tonight with her pals. It was going to be the best Halloween ever!

Chapter Fifteen

"Wait a minute, little miss. First, you were going out trick-or-treating with Frances, then you weren't, and now you are?" her mom questioned, setting a bowl of spaghetti on the lazy Susan.

"Right," Allie said, tying a tea towel around her neck and sitting down to the dinner table. She'd removed the cracked egg, the feather wings, and the hat of her costume, but she didn't want to take the chance of getting red sauce on her sweater or tights.

"So, I don't need to drive you?" her dad asked.

"Nope."

"I thought Frances's dad had something else to do."

Allie took a deep breath and sighed dramatically. "Look, things kinda got mixed up because Frances and I had a fight."

Her mom set a bowl of green salad on the table. "A fight? You and Frances never fight."

"Well, we did."

"What was it about?"

Allie wasn't about to spill the beans about Frances's mom saying that her mom didn't have time for Halloween costumes or bake sales. Instead, she just shrugged and said, "Ah, nothing important. Some stupid thing, I can't even remember. But we made up at school and now everything's good."

Stephanie came quietly into the kitchen and sat down. Mom ignored her.

"Hi, Miss Stephanie!" Dad said.

"Hi, Dad."

"Your mom said you wanted to talk to me about your science club."

"Oh, that's okay. We can talk later. It's just about fund-raising. Boring dinner conversation."

Dad went back to reading his paper. "Okay, you just let me know."

"Oh, don't worry, Dad, we will definitely be talking."

Allie knew what that talk would be about, and it had nothing to do with fund-raising. Allie wondered if her dad would really listen to what Stephanie had to say about Paul, or if he'd just minimize everything like Mom did. She didn't want Paul to get in trouble, but she didn't want him running around with that Mike kid, either.

Mom set a plate of garlic bread on the table and sat down. She glanced over at Stephanie. "I think we should say grace tonight. Stephanie?"

Stephanie glowered at the garlic bread.

Dad put down his paper. "Stephanie? Your mother asked you to say grace."

Allie held her breath, waiting for Stephanie to say "Grace" in her most obnoxious voice. Nothing else—just the word "Grace."

"Fine," she grumbled. "Dear Lord, we are grateful for this food. Please bless it. And bless Paul, wherever he is. Amen."

"Where is he, by the way?" Dad asked, after his "amen."

"He went to the library to study," Mom answered, turning the lazy Susan so that Dad could have first dibs on the spaghetti.

"Really?" Stephanie said in her fake sweet voice. "He went to the library on Halloween? Isn't that great of him? Wow, he's really taking your grounding to heart, isn't he?"

"Stephanie, that's enough," Mom warned.

"What?" Stephanie asked, giving her mom a wide-eyed, innocent look. "I'm impressed by my big brother's behavior. It's admirable."

"What's that mean?" Allie asked, after taking a big bite of garlic bread

"Don't talk with your mouth full," Mom said.

Stephanie put salad on her plate. "It means, little sis, that Paul is doing great things to make Mom and Dad proud."

Dad frowned at her, and Allie slunk back into her chair. "Stephanie, why the sarcasm?"

"Sorry, Dad. I won't say another word."

Allie stopped chewing, as the room had suddenly gone very quiet, and she didn't want to bring attention to herself.

Dad leaned forward. "Do you have something to say about your brother?"

"No. Not a thing. Let's just eat dinner so we can all have a fun Halloween night."

"I want my cloud hat," Trudy said from her table. Mom stood and went to fetch it.

"I'm glad your costume won a prize," Stephanie said.

Allie nearly choked on her bread at the abrupt change of topic. "Really?"

"Yeah. It's cute."

"Thanks, Steph."

"You're welcome."

Allie dished herself some spaghetti and turned the lazy Susan toward Stephanie. She leaned closer to her sister. "You're right, ya know," she whispered. "Paul is up to something."

"Allie, it's not polite to whisper."

Allie sat straight up in her chair. "Sorry, Dad, we were just talking about Halloween."

"Not my favorite holiday," Mom said, returning to the table.

"Not my favorite holiday," Trudy repeated.

"For good reason," Mom concurred. "Kids banging on the door and yelling 'trick or treat' all night? It's enough to give someone a nervous headache."

"Well, it'll all be over in a couple of hours," Allie said.

"And then you'll have enough candy to last for months," Stephanie said, smiling.

Allie smiled back and gave her two thumbs up, but then Mom said, "Another reason I don't like it—all that sugar will rot your teeth."

Allie's smile vanished. She glanced over at Trudy's table and seriously considered joining her.

* * *

As Allie stepped into her cracked egg and brought the suspenders over her shoulders, she breathed a sigh of relief. Spaghetti dinner was normally one of her favorites, but not tonight. She had found it hard to swallow more than a couple of bites, as the bread and spaghetti had a wrestling match in her stomach. Mom said she didn't eat because she was too excited about running wild in the neighborhood. *Maybe,* Allie thought, *or maybe it is because of worry for my dumb brother.*

Stephanie came into her room.

"Can I help?"

"Ah...sure." Allie chocked. She wondered why Stephanie was being so nice. Normally she made Allie feel like she was an irritation or gum on the bottom of her shoe.

Stephanie handed her the feather cap, and Allie put it on.

"Stick out your arms," her sister said, and Allie did as she was told. Stephanie tied on the fluffy yellow wings, then came around the front to check out the look. "Cute." She stepped closer. "Now, tell me what you know about that blue and white car."

"Huh?"

"You heard me. That blue and white car that almost crashed our bus."

Allie stepped back. "I... It's just some car..."

"Don't tell me it's just some car you've seen around."

"Gee, Steph. What's your problem? Why are you so bugged about this car?"

"Because I think it has something to do with Paul." She took hold of Allie's wrist. "So, spill it."

The doorbell rang, and Allie pulled free. "That's Mr. Catera! He's come to pick me up!"

"Hang on."

Allie backed away. "I can't, Steph!" The doorbell rang a second time. "I gotta go!" She grabbed her candy bucket and headed to the door. "I'll talk to you later."

"Count on it."

Allie raced down the stairs and nearly bumped into her dad, who was talking to Mr. Catera at the door.

"I plan to have the girls home around eight thirty, Alan."

"Okay, Norman, that'll be great."

"Bye, Dad."

"Bye, Chicken Little. Have fun. Stay out of trouble."

"Daaaad." Allie stepped out into the cold night and was grateful for her thick sweater. She saw Frances and Sharon waving at the windows. She ran to the car, and Sharon opened the back door.

"Trick-or-treat!" Sharon called, sliding over and letting Allie in. "We're going to have so much fun!"

"*Peep, peep, peep*," Allie said, and the three friends laughed together. She shut the door and turned to wave good-bye to her dad, as Mr. Catera got in and started the car.

"Where to, girls?" he said cheerily.

"To the candy!" Frances shouted.

"To the candy, it is!" Mr. Catera declared as he pulled out into the dark night.

Allie was sure this was going to be the best Halloween ever.

* * *

"Okay, girls, about time to go home," Mr. Catera said as he pulled over and parked the car by the side of the road. "Just this one last stop and then home, okay?"

"Okay, Dad, but this is the stop we've been waiting for," Frances said, peering out the car window.

Mr. Catera grinned and nodded. "I know, the fancy houses."

"Exactly!"

"Okay. You hit one side of the street and then come back on the opposite side. I'll wait for you here."

"Great! Thanks, Dad!" Frances said, getting out of the car.

"Yes, thank you, Mr. Catera," Sharon said as she joined her.

Mr. Catera chuckled. "Your buckets are nearly filled to the top already. Where are you going to fit more candy?"

"Oh, we'll find a way," Allie said.

"I'm sure you will." Allie slammed the back door, and Mr. Catera rolled down his window. "Frances, I can come with you. It's really dark."

"No, Dad. We're fine. Look, all the houses have their lights on, and there are other kids still running around."

Mr. Catera hesitated. "Well, don't be long."

"Okay!" the three girls chorused as they raced off to the nearest house.

Allie loved these homes that overlooked the meadow. Most were owned by bankers and doctors. "Prime real estate" her dad called it, whatever that meant. To Allie it meant full-sized candy bars on Halloween night. Sure enough—house one, full-sized Almond Joys. House two, full-sized Milky Way bars. House three, fat packages of homemade fudge! The girls couldn't stop whooping each time the door closed behind them and they were off to their next conquest. The next fancy house had its lights off, which, in trick-or-treating etiquette, meant the people weren't home or they'd run out of candy. The girls groaned.

"Oh well, Frances said. "We still have the other side of the street."

"What about Mrs. Hemmett's house?" Allie asked slowly.

"The witch woman's house?" Frances squeaked.

"She's not a witch," Allie said. "And look, her front porch light is on, so she must want trick-or-treaters to come by."

"I'm afraid of what kind of treat we'd get," Sharon said.

"Me, too," Frances said.

"Oh, don't be babies. I've been inside her house and it's fine. A couple of times she's even tried to give me Oreos."

Sharon pulled her heavy cloak closer around her body. "Well, it would be kinda cool telling everyone we went to creepy Mrs. Hemmett's house on Halloween."

Allie looked over. "Frances?"

Frances bit her bottom lip and stomped her feet. "Well...well, I don't know."

"Come on," Allie said. "It'll be better than standing around freezing." She started toward the house and Sharon followed.

Frances hesitated and then ran to catch up. "Well, okay, but don't blame me if we get some sort of poisoned apples or chocolate-covered beetles for the treat."

The stairs creaked as they walked up onto the porch, and Allie felt a cold wind on the back of her neck.

"Did you feel that?" Frances whispered.

"Yes, it was the hand of death passing by," Sharon said.

"Not funny, Sharon!" Frances yelped.

Allie reached to knock on the door. "Now, nobody freak out when you see her face. Some stupid doctor didn't know how to sew it up right after a car accident."

"Um...maybe this wasn't such a good idea," Sharon said, taking a step back.

Allie knocked. No answer. She knocked again.

"Let's go," Frances pleaded. "She's not home."

"She's always home. Listen, someone's coming!"

Frances started whining, and Sharon took another step back. The door opened.

"Trick-or-treat!" said only Allie's voice.

"Is that Allie Whitman?" came Mrs. Hemmett's gravelly voice through the screen door.

"It is, Mrs. Hemmett. I'm here with my friends Frances and Sharon."

"Well, how nice. How nice. Let me see your costumes." The girls bunched together as Mrs. Hemmett opened the screen door. Allie held her breath, hoping her friends wouldn't shriek or scream. They actually did pretty well. Frances only gave a slight whimper, and Sharon's Cleopatra eyes widened, but neither of them ran off the porch or fainted.

"Frances and I are chicks coming out of our eggs, and Sharon is..."

"Cleopatra, of course. Very good costumes. Wonderful."

"We won prizes at the costume parade."

"I can see why."

Allie was amazed at how she was just chatting away with Horrible Hemmett. Maybe it was because it was Halloween and she was prepared for spooky and scary things. Or maybe it was because she'd used Mrs. Hemmett's bathroom, and once you've used someone's bathroom, you could sort of see the person as normal.

"Hold on a second, and I'll get your treats."

Mrs. Hemmett stepped into her house and came out with a big bowl of *something*—big round balls wrapped in waxed paper and tied with black and orange ribbon. The thought of wrapped animal heads flashed through Allie's mind. She scolded herself.

"Wow, Mrs. Hemmett! What are those?"

"Chewy caramel popcorn balls."

Frances reached out immediately. "I love those!"

"These are the best. They're my mother's recipe."

Sharon and Allie both reached for one.

"Take two," Mrs. Hemmett said, holding out the bowl to them.

"Really?" Frances asked, already with another one in her hand.

"Go ahead and take three or four. You're the only ones brave enough to come up here—you might as well be rewarded." The girls were having a hard time figuring out where to put all their treasure. "Here, let me go get a paper bag and we'll just dump them all in." Mrs. Hemmett turned back into the house and the screen door banged.

"Wow!" Sharon said. "I'm glad we came here."

"Me, too," Allie agreed.

"Even if she is scary," Sharon whispered.

"Yeah, she is scary," Frances said, squinting to see through the rusted screen door. "But I love caramel popcorn balls!"

"We can tell," Sharon said, laughing.

Mrs. Hemmett returned with the bag. She had Allie hold it and was just dumping in the treats when car lights raked across her front porch. There was the squeal of brakes and the sound of car doors opening.

"Hey, Hemmett!" a slurred voice called out. "Horrible rotten Hemmett!" The high-pitched sound of something being thrown whizzed past Allie's ear, then whatever it was smashed into the side of Mrs. Hemmett's house.

The girls screamed, and Mrs. Hemmett swore.

"This is your night, huh? The night of freaks and ghouls," came the voice again, followed by waves of male laughter, and more projectiles.

"They're throwing eggs!" Sharon yelled.

"Girls, get into the house!" Mrs. Hemmett commanded, turning to shepherd them to safety.

"Look! She's trying to kill those kids!" came a different slurred voice.

An egg hit Mrs. Hemmett on the back of the head and knocked her to her knees. The laughter rang out again. The girls ran to help her.

"It's okay, it's okay," Mrs. Hemmett said groggily, trying to rise. "You girls get in the house."

Another egg flew and hit her in the back.

"Good shot, Mike!"

Allie stiffened. Mike! It was that punk kid, Mike. She lost all sense of reason. She ran to the edge of the porch.

"No! Don't!" Mrs. Hemmett yelled.

"Leave her alone! I know you! Stupid punk—Mike! I know you, and I'm gonna tell my dad!"

An egg missed her head by an inch and smashed into the front window.

"Allie, come here!" Mrs. Hemmett shouted.

"Yeah? You better leave those girls alone, Hemmett, or I'll smash your head in with this tire iron."

Allie stumbled back. She couldn't see the punk because of the car lights in her face, but she could tell his voice was coming closer.

"Mike, that's enough!" came another slurred voice. There was a grunt and the sound of the tire iron hitting the bottom step.

"Get off of me!"

"I said enough! Let's get outta here!"

"I said, get off of me!"

There was the sound of a struggle—grunts, punches, swearing. The car lights went off, and for a moment Allie couldn't see anything. Then she saw two guys fighting and two others trying to break them up and drag them back to the car.

Car lights were coming toward them down the road. Mike grabbed the tire iron and took one last swing at his buddy, grazing him across the forehead. The guy groaned and fell to the ground with a thud. The guy lay without moving as the other three raced for the car, jumped in, and skidded off down the road in the opposite direction from the oncoming car.

"It's my dad!" Frances cried. She jumped up and down and waved her arms above her head. Tears streamed down her face. "It's my dad!"

Mr. Catera pulled into Mrs. Hemmett's front yard, slamming on his brakes when he saw the body lying on the ground. He got out quickly and Frances ran over to him, flinging her arms around his waist. "What in the world is going on here?" he demanded.

Mrs. Hemmett came off the porch, and Allie and Sharon came with her. Allie glanced over at Mrs. Hemmett's face and saw anger and concern, but she also saw fear. What was she afraid of? Surly she didn't think Mr. Catera would blame her for anything.

"What happened here?" Mr. Catera barked.

"A gang of boys decided to egg my house. The girls got in their way. I'm sorry."

Allie frowned. What did she have to be sorry about?

Mr. Catera motioned to Allie and Sharon. "Girls, come here." They walked over to him, and he looked directly at them. "Are you two all right?"

"Yes, sir," they said together.

"What in the world were you doing here?"

"Trick-or-treating," Allie said.

"Here?"

Allie frowned. "Yeah, why not?"

"So, this was your idea?"

"Yes, sir," Allie said slowly.

"I should have known."

Allie's anger resurfaced. "What does that mean?"

"Mind your manners, young lady. Now, all three of you go get in the car."

Frances and Sharon complied, but Allie turned toward the porch.

"Where are you going?" Mr. Catera asked.

"To get my trick-or-treating stuff."

"Don't forget the paper bag," Frances said quietly.

"Into the car...now!" Mr. Catera said sharply.

Allie retrieved her candy bucket and the bag and headed back to the car. She wouldn't look at the punk kid on the ground, because he wasn't moving and maybe he was dead, and she didn't want to see a dead person, especially on Halloween night. She slid into the back seat of the car and moved close to her friends. Frances was still crying, and Sharon was absently staring at the candy in her bucket.

"I'm sorry, you guys," Allie said. It was all she could do not to cry.

"Wasn't your fault," Sharon said.

"Yes, it was. I was the one who wanted to go to Mrs. Hemmett's place."

"But everything was great until those hoodlums showed up."

"Yeah, we got a whole bag of caramel corn balls," Frances said, wiping her face on the sleeve of her sweater.

Allie put her arm around her friends' shoulders. "You guys are so great."

Suddenly Sharon sat forward and stared out the front window. "Uh-oh. Frances, your dad's getting that punk kid up off the ground. The guy looks drunk."

Frances sat up so she could see over the front seat. "What? Why's my dad doing that? That guy could punch him or something."

"Don't worry," Allie said. "There's a police car coming down the road. One of the neighbors must have called the cops."

"Yes!" Frances cheered, tears forgotten. "Now that guy's gonna get it!"

The police car stopped, and two uniformed men got out. The girls hunched together when they passed by. As they approached Mr. Catera, he turned the boy around to face the officers, and the girls finally got a look at his face. They all gasped.

"Oh no," Frances said in a mewling voice. "I think I'm gonna be sick. Look at that blood on his face."

"We see it. We see it," Sharon said impatiently. She elbowed Allie. "Ah, Allie... Isn't that your brother?"

"What?" Allie whispered. She leaned forward and squinted her eyes. *It can't be my brother. He's at the library studying.*

Chapter Sixteen

Pastor Kline was deep into his sermon about Jonah and the whale, and Allie sat frowning at him and questioning the whole idea of a man living inside a big fish. It was interesting, but not very likely. She thought back to when she'd seen the Disney movie *Pinocchio*, and how sad she was that the wooden boy and his dad were trapped inside mean old Monstro. She had been captivated by the cartoon and believed the frightful occurrence without question. Of course, she was only in second grade at the time.

Allie opened her youth Bible and found the picture of poor old Jonah being tossed off a boat into an angry sea. It seemed like a mean thing to do to an old man. She sighed and looked over at the stained-glass picture of Mary and the baby Jesus. She was pretty sure Jesus wouldn't throw anybody off a boat. In fact, she remembered a story of Peter falling in the water and Jesus lifting him up. She flipped through the pages looking for that picture.

"Stop fidgeting," Stephanie whispered, giving her a pinch.

"Ow! I'm not fidgeting!

"Yes, you are."

Allie scowled at her, and Stephanie threatened another pinch. Allie slumped back into the pew. She hated their new seating arrangement. It was still Mom, Tru, and Dad, but now Paul sat next to Dad and Stephanie sat next to her. And she was still at the far end, as usual.

"So, what did the prophet Jonah learn from this experience?" Pastor Kline asked the congregation.

No one said anything, of course, because one, it was rude to talk out loud in church, and two, they knew he was going to give them the answer anyway, so why bother?

"Well, I believe he learned many things. He learned to honor, trust, and obey the Lord. He also learned that the people of Nineveh, who were pagans and his enemies, were also precious to the Lord."

Allie frowned. She would have to look up the word pagans in her dictionary when she got home, but she figured it was something like *sinners*.

Pastor Kline's voice grew in intensity. "Yes, they were pagans, and yes, they were sinners, but still they were precious to the Lord. They deserved the chance to be saved. They deserved the chance to hear a prophet speak to them, and to call them to repentance. They deserved the chance to feel the love of God in their lives."

Paul stood, shoved his way past Stephanie and Allie, and left the chapel. Dad stood to follow, but Mom leaned over and caught his wrist. "No, Alan." He sat back down.

Allie glanced over at Stephanie, but she was frowning at Pastor Kline like she had X-ray vision—irritated X-ray vision. Was she angry at Pastor Kline for talking about Jonah? Did she think it was his fault that Paul had left the meeting? Maybe she was just trying to avoid the looks from some members of the congregation. Allie saw Old Widow McCabe shaking her head at them, so she stuck out her tongue at her. The woman gave a little hiccup and turned her attention to the pastor.

Allie flipped through the pages of her Bible until she found the picture of Jesus sitting on the sunny hillside teaching a bunch of people. The grass was filled with wildflowers, and the look on Jesus' face was kind. Allie figured nobody ever stood up and left one of *His* sermons. She studied the picture and thought about her brother's exit from the church. Maybe the stiches in his head were hurting. Maybe he had to go to the bathroom. Maybe he was tired of people talk-talk-talking—including Dad and Mom asking him a hundred questions and trying to get to the bottom of things.

That Halloween night, while Paul was getting patched up at the clinic, Mom stood in front of him with her arms folded, not saying a word. Dad sat in the hallway with his head leaned back against the wall and his eyes closed. Stephanie had taken Tru down the hall to look for a vending machine. She'd invited Allie to come along, but Allie had chosen to stay and watch the doctor stitch. She stood at the open office door, wincing every time the doctor put the needle into Paul's skin. At the end of the process, while the doctor was at the supply cabinet getting bandages, Paul had thrown up, and Allie was surprised that her mom stepped away from him, not giving him any kind words or offering any help. In fact, she'd let the nurse sponge the vomit off Paul's pants, and she moved back to stand by the wall while the orderly mopped the floor. Paul looked so miserable that Allie wanted to go and hold his hand, but she didn't dare bring attention to herself.

After that night, Mom had a lot of words and questions. Paul had a lot of excuses and anger. Stephanie had a lot of opinions and observations, and Dad took a lot of Alka-Seltzer. Allie stayed in her room and wore earmuffs so she couldn't hear the fighting. So, she didn't hear Paul spilling the truth about Halloween night, when he and his punk friends drank a keg of beer and then went out to terrorize Mrs. Hemmett. She also didn't hear him apologize a hundred times and promise never to go out drinking again. In the days following the confession and the apology, there wasn't a lot of yelling, but there wasn't a lot of laughter, either.

The first notes from the organ made Allie jump and brought her mind into the chapel, where everyone was standing for the closing song. She held one side of the hymnal while Stephanie held the other, but when her family and the rest of the congregation started singing, Allie didn't join in. She didn't feel like singing, or praying, or saying "amen." She trudged down the aisle at the end of the service, and out of the church into the snowy afternoon. She hunched into her coat, dreading the silent car ride and the cold feeling waiting at home with Dad's quietness and Mom's anger at the whole world—the whole world except Trudy.

Allie sat sullenly in the back seat, staring out the window as the snow swirled past, trying to imagine herself on that green hillside with wildflowers. She glanced over at Paul, who was staring out his window, and suddenly she realized something! She realized that even though she and Paul were pagan sinners, Jesus would still let them sit on that hillside in the sunshine and listen to His stories.

Chapter Seventeen

If normal tension could be cut with a knife, Allie figured the tension in the car Monday afternoon could be cut with a chainsaw. She sat in the back seat with the laundry baskets while Paul sat in the front with Mom—both of them looking like mannequins.

Allie watched the cold sleet coming down and shivered. "Mom, could you turn on the heat?"

"We'll be there in a second."

Paul grunted, and Mom turned to scowl at him.

"What? You have an opinion on this?"

"No."

"Well, I would hope not." She pulled into Mrs. Hemmett's yard and turned off the engine. "Okay, everybody out." Paul sat unmoving. "I mean it, Paul."

"Don't you think this weather has probably washed all the egg away by now?"

Mom opened her car door. "Out. Now."

Allie got quickly out of the car and reached for her basket of laundry.

"Paul will get that."

Paul shoved open his door, stepped out into a slushy puddle, and swore. Allie held her breath, waiting for Mom's reprimand, but it didn't come.

Choosing her battles, Allie thought. That's what her dad had taught her about disagreements. It takes too much energy to fight about everything, so he said to choose the things that really counted and let the other stuff go. "Discretionary fighting," he'd called it, and that night Allie had put the word *discretionary* in the back of her diary. Of course, her dad hardly fought about anything. Allie wondered if there was a word for that.

"Step aside, Squirt," Paul said as he moved to get the basket. "Off to face Horrible Hemmett."

Allie flinched. Her mean title for Mabel Hemmett didn't seem to fit anymore, and she didn't like Paul saying it in such a nasty tone. What right did he have to call her names? She didn't go to *his* house on Halloween night and throw eggs. Allie thought she might start calling her brother Putrid Paul.

"Come on, you two!" Mom called back moving toward the front porch.

Paul slammed the car door. "It's really starting to snow!" he yelled to her, but she ignored him and kept walking.

As the three climbed onto the porch, Mrs. Hemmett was already there with the door open. "Saw you three coming."

"Thanks, Mabel," Mom said, handing over her basket.

Mrs. Hemmett took it and set it inside the house. "Brought the boy along," she said, taking his crate. "How's the head?"

Paul glanced up, then back down at his shoes. "Hurts."

"I'd imagine."

"He has something to say to you, Mabel."

"Oh?"

"Go on, Paul."

"Sorry about the other night," Paul mumbled, not looking at her.

"What's that?"

"Paul, speak up," Mom said sharply.

Paul looked up, and Allie noted that there was no sorry in his face.

"I'm sorry about Halloween night. We were just having a little fun."

"I see."

"And?" Mom prompted.

"And I want to clean up the mess."

"The eggs, you mean?" Mrs. Hemmett asked.

"Yeah, the eggs."

"I'll get a bucket of hot water and a scrub brush." She looked at Mrs. Whitman and Allie. "You want to wait in the house?"

"Ah, no. No thank you, Mabel. We'll wait in the car."

"Suit yourself."

When Mrs. Hemmett moved off to get the cleaning supplies, Mom stepped over to Paul. "Do a good job." He didn't respond. She frowned at him and shook her head. "I don't understand what's gotten into you." She turned to Allie. "Come on, before you catch your death."

"Yeah, I'm freezing."

"Well, why did you wear that stupid lightweight jacket?"

Just like Paul, Allie didn't answer. She snugged the collar of the stupid lightweight jacket around her neck and trudged after her mom to the car. She climbed into the front seat to be nearer to the vents in case, by a miracle, her mom decided to turn on the heater.

Allie squinted to see what Paul was doing, but snow was accumulating on the front windshield, making it difficult to see more than a blob of movement. Just then her mom turned on the car and the windshield wipers sprang into action, causing Allie to jump. A trickle of heat came out of the old Ford's heating system, and Allie sighed. Well, at least she'd be saved from frostbite. Mom turned off the wipers, but luckily the few swipes had cleared a good lookout to the scene on the porch. Mrs. Hemmett was back with the bucket and brush. She handed them to Paul and pointed out the places where the egg goop had hardened. Paul turned toward her front window and started working. Allie figured Mrs. Hemmett would retreat into the house to get out of the cold, but she didn't; she stayed where she was, arms folded across her chest, talking away to her captive audience. *Weird.* Allie couldn't hear what she was saying, but it seemed Paul was mostly ignoring her.

Allie looked over at her mom to see if she was observing this strange scene, but she found her working on the checkbook. Her father had turned over the balancing of the checkbook to her mom when Allie was eight. She well remembered the heated discussion at breakfast that historic day.

"I can't do it, Alan."

"Of course, you can, Patricia. You are a very capable woman."

"Oh! For heaven's sake! That's not what I meant. I can't because I have too much to do already. I can't add one more thing to my list."

"It doesn't take that much time, if you keep up with it."

"I don't want to keep up with it. You're the CPA; you keep up with it."

"I feel it's important for you to know how to do this, Patricia."

"Well, I don't."

"Well, I do. Listen, I'll take over one of your household chores if you'll do it."

Allie remembered that Mom went silent at that point, as she slid a plate of burned toast and overcooked eggs in front of him. "Clean the toilets?"

"Done."

"Okay."

Allie focused back on Paul just as he moved to scrub a crusted patch by the door. Mrs. Hemmett kept talking, and Allie squinted, wishing she could read lips.

"I wonder what she's talking about?" she mumbled.

Her mom frowned over at her. "What's that?"

"Huh?"

"What did you say?"

"Did I say that out loud?"

"Well, you mumbled something."

"Oh."

"So, what was it?"

"I just wondered what Mrs. Hemmett is saying to Paul."

"To Paul?" Her mom flicked on the windshield wipers and peered at the scene. "That's odd."

"Maybe she's telling him how to clean up the eggs," Allie offered.

"That's ridiculous. He doesn't need instruction on how to do that."

Allie shrugged. "It's her house."

"Don't be sassy."

Paul knelt on the soggy porch, attacking the last egg with such force that Allie figured he was gouging a hole in the wood. "Wow! He seems pretty mad about whatever it is that she's saying."

The two watched silently as Paul stood, threw the brush hard onto the porch, and kicked over the bucket. The water sloshed onto Mrs. Hemmett's shoes.

"What in the world?" her mom said, shoving open the car door and stepping out into the sleet.

Paul's long legs carried him quickly down the steps and across the yard. "Let's get out of here."

"What happened?"

Paul reached the car. "Never mind. Let's just go." He slid into the back seat and slammed the door.

Mom got in, too. "Should I talk to her?"

"No! Definitely not. Just drive."

Mom put the car into reverse. "Well, you're going to have to tell me what happened, Paul."

"She's crazy, that's all."

Allie watched Mrs. Hemmett as the car turned off toward the street. She was picking up the bucket and brush and shaking her head. She didn't look crazy, just sad.

"I don't think you should go there anymore," Paul said suddenly.

"Why not?"

"Because she's creepy, and her house is creepy."

Into Allie's mind popped images of clean polished floors and a spotless bathroom. *Nothing creepy about that.*

"And she buries dead animals in her backyard, Mom. Maybe there are other dead things there, too—not just animals."

"Paul, for heaven's sake. Stop it. Now, tell me what she said to you." Paul hesitated, and Mom gave him one of her "do it now" looks.

"Okay, but you're not going to like it."

"Spill it."

"She told me all about the car accident. The one that mangled up her face."

"Gross," Allie said. "Why would she do that?"

"Allie, be quiet!" Mom snapped. She turned to Paul. "Why would she do that?"

"I don't know. And it seemed like she really enjoyed telling me all the gory details."

Allie was feeling kind of queasy. "That's sick."

Paul looked back at her. "I know, it is sick. That's why I got so angry." His focus shifted to their mom. "And that's why I don't think you should go there anymore. You never know what might happen."

"Paul, stop. Mabel Hemmett may be a recluse and a bit odd, but she is not dangerous."

"Well, ya never know. She might be on the verge of a break-down or something."

Mom didn't speak for several blocks, and then she shook her head. "I'll talk to your father and then decide."

"Okay, but if you want my opinion..."

"I've heard your opinion, Paul. Now, that's enough."

And that was that. Allie knew when Mom spoke the word "enough," any conversation was over. Paul slumped into a sullen silence, and Allie turned to the storm outside her window. She breathed on the glass, causing a cloudy background for artwork. She traced out a face: eyes, nose, mouth, and lumpy skin with a scar. She stared at her creation for a moment, thinking about the sad look on Mrs. Hemmett's face as she'd picked up the brush and bucket. Allie reached over and swiped her hand across the image. The scarred face disappeared.

Chapter Eighteen

Allie turned over and snuggled her head into her pillow, slowly becoming aware of a special silence—the silence of snow! Her eyes opened a slit and she smiled. Groggily she pushed aside her covers and stumbled out of bed to the window, finding the glass frosted with sparkling crystals and the ground and pine trees outside covered in a magical blanket of white. The first real snow of the winter! All the prior storms had left slushy dabs of snow that washed away with the rain or melted by the afternoon, but Allie knew this one would stick.

She heard movement and voices downstairs and ran to put on her bathrobe and slippers. Midway down the stairs she saw a cheery fire in the fireplace; she also noticed that Mom and Dad had moved Trudy's table and chair in front of the big picture window in the living room. The eight-year-old was sitting calmly with her hand on the barometer, gazing out at the winter wonderland. Allie moved quietly to her side.

"Morning, Tru."

"Morning."

"Wow!" Allie whispered.

"Wow," Trudy answered. "Let's sing 'Suzy Snowflake'."

Allie was shocked. She had sung the song to her sister last winter, and after three times of Trudy saying "again" she had sung along. But that was a year ago and Allie was sure she wouldn't remember it.

"Do you want me to sing it for you first?"

"No."

"Okay, here we go."

"Where are we going?"

"I mean we're going to sing now."

"Okay."

"Here comes Suzy Snowflake dressed in a snow-white gown,

"Tap tap tapping at your windowpane to tell you she's in town.

"Here comes Suzy Snowflake dressed in a snow-white gown,

"Tap tap tapping at your windowpane to tell you she's in town."

"Well done, girls."

Allie turned to see her dad standing in the kitchen doorway and smiling. "Thanks, Dad." She knew he hadn't clapped because it would have upset Trudy, but the warm tone in his voice was ten times better than clapping. "Can you believe she remembered? It's amazing!"

"It is, indeed," her dad said, nodding. He gave Allie a wink. "You about ready for breakfast?"

Allie held her stomach and groaned. "Yes, I'm starving!"

"The only children starving are the children in China!" her mom called from the kitchen.

Mr. Whitman raised his eyebrows, and Allie stood straighter. "Well, I'm really hungry," she mumbled. "Can't I be hungry?"

"Of course, I'm hungry, too," he said as he walked over to Trudy. "Mom's making French toast, would you like to try a piece?"

She didn't look at him. "No. I don't like French toast or American toast. A banana, please."

Allie saw her dad grin. "A banana?" He put his hand gently on Trudy's shoulder. "I'll tell your mom."

Paul came racing down the stairs at that moment, smiling and humming. "Man, breakfast smells good." He ruffled Allie's hair. "Morning, Squirt. Morning, Dad." He walked over to Trudy's table. "Morning, Tru."

"Well, somebody's in a good mood this morning," Dad said.

"It's Saturday, and I'm going with Jennifer Green to do a little Christmas shopping! Who wouldn't be in a good mood?" Paul said, heading for the kitchen. He met Allie in the door frame and pretended they were stuck. "Hey, little sis! Have you gained weight or something?"

Allie giggled and pushed against him. "Just 'cause you're the size of a rhino." They finally popped through into the kitchen, and Allie batted him on the arm. "Stupid brother." She liked having the old Paul back. It seemed that Mom did, too, as Allie caught her smiling at him and shaking her head.

"Oh, for heaven's sake, settle down and eat before it gets cold."

"I don't have to be told twice," Paul said, scooting out his chair and sitting. He rubbed his hands together as he surveyed the food. "Man, oh man, Mom, this is some layout!"

Allie had to agree. There were stacks of French toast and piles of sausages, along with warm banana bread and sliced oranges.

Dad came in and gave his wife a hug. "Morning, again."

"Morning again to you."

"Trudy wants a banana."

"Really?"

"Yep. That's what she requested. I can take it to her."

"No, I'll do it." She handed her husband the spatula. "If you can just turn those last four pieces of toast."

"I think I can manage."

Mom grabbed a banana and headed over to Trudy's table.

"Can we start eating?" Allie called after her.

"Of course."

"Yes!" She picked up her fork and skewered a sausage, taking a bite before putting it on her plate.

"Hey! Mind your manners," Paul said, picking up a fat piece of French toast and shoving half of it into his mouth.

Allie laughed. "You'd better not let Mom catch you doing that."

"Yeah, right?" He put the piece of French toast carefully on his plate. "I'm just now getting back into her good graces."

Allie nodded. She knew that was true. For the past couple of weeks, she had watched her brother trying to be the perfect son. He wasn't wasting time with his football buddies, but instead was doing extra homework, housework, and wood stacking. He hadn't been swearing, or walking out of church, or yelling at anybody. And it seemed his angelic behavior had paid off, because Mom gave him the honor of laying the wreath on Grandpa Harrison's grave for Veterans' Day. Allie sighed as she buttered her French toast. Yep, it seemed like the "punk Mike days" were behind them. She was glad. For one thing, when Paul was being so awful, Allie was afraid he'd forget their secret promise and spill the beans about her digging up Mr. Stubbs. If Mom knew *that* truth, Allie could see herself sliding down the ladder of Mom's affection below her Aunt Edna and Aunt Evelyn, or maybe even below some of Mom's friends at the PTA. No, with Paul happy, her secret would be safe. For another thing, with Paul happy, there was a lot less tension in the house, and Allie liked things calm. Yep. Everything seemed to be back to normal. Well, normal except that they weren't taking special laundry to Mrs. Hemmett's place anymore. Mom had decided that she could do it with the other laundry just fine for a while, but Allie noticed that it wasn't fine. It wasn't nearly as good as Mrs. Hemmett's work by a long shot. Dad and Paul's Sunday white shirts looked sorta gray, the Sunday tablecloth still had a gravy stain, and Trudy refused to wear some of her dresses. She said they were "crunchy."

Mom came into the kitchen as Dad was putting the final pieces of French toast on the serving platter.

"Thanks, Alan."

"You're welcome. I also put your English muffin in the toaster." He picked up the coffeepot. "Coffee?"

"Of course." She brought the platter to the lazy Susan and sat down.

"Mom?"

"Yes, Allie?"

"Where's Stephanie?"

"Sleeping. She's not feeling well."

"Ah, that's too bad," Paul said, a forkful of food paused halfway to his mouth. "I hope it's nothing serious."

Allie didn't believe his concern for one minute, but Mom seemed to be buying it.

"We don't know yet. She did have a cough and a high temperature at six this morning."

"Wow, that's too bad." He shoved the forkful of food into his mouth and moaned happily.

Mom grinned at him. "Well, you obviously haven't lost your appetite over it."

"I can be starving and concerned at the same time, can't I?"

"The only people who are starving are in China," Allie piped up.

There was silence for a moment, and then everyone laughed. Allie smiled and sat up straighter. It was nice to have the family happy again.

Mom's English muffin popped up, and she went to get it. "I just hope she's not sick for Thanksgiving."

"That's this week, isn't it?" Allie said excitedly.

"It is," her dad replied. "And I can't wait—turkey, and stuffing, and potatoes."

"And marshmallow yams, and pumpkin pie!" Allie added.

Mom came back to the table. "My goodness, you're all just fixated on your stomachs, aren't you?"

"Fixated? Good word. What's it mean?" Allie asked.

"It means we can't think of anything else but food, food, food," her dad said, laughing.

"Well, it's Thanksgiving! What do you expect?"

"I expect that you'd give a little thought to how Stephanie's feeling. It's terrible to be sick over a holiday," Mom said buttering her English muffin.

That's true, Allie thought. She remembered the time she had tonsillitis for the Fourth of July and missed the Rotary Club picnic, the fireworks, and her mom's deep-fried doughnuts.

"Sorry, Mom. You're right. I'll say a prayer that she's not sick for Thanksgiving."

Mom gave her a look like she didn't know who she was looking at. "Well, good. That would be a good thing to do."

"I can do something nice for her, too!" Paul said. "Dad, can I borrow the car for a few hours?"

"How's that doing a nice thing for your sister?"

"Well, I can take Jennifer Green Christmas shopping, and at the same time I can buy a little something for Steph. That would cheer her up."

Mom took a bite of her English muffin and shook her head. "Charm the birds out of the trees, right?"

Dad winked at her, then turned to Paul. "Well, you have been bringing your grades up and working hard around here. I suppose you deserve a little time off from your grounding." He got the keys out of his pocket and handed them to Paul. "Wait for the plows to clear the roads first."

"I will. Thanks, Dad."

"And you'll have to shovel the driveway."

"No problem."

"And drive like your mother."

Paul grimaced. "Really? It'll take me an hour just to get to Jennifer's house!"

Mom swatted him on the arm with the tea towel. "That's enough of that."

Paul burst out laughing. "Just kidding. I'll be careful."

"Mom, can I watch Saturday morning cartoons?" Allie asked, figuring she might get away with something, too, since everybody was in such a good mood.

No such luck. "After breakfast and chores," her mom answered simply. She stood and poured a glass of apple juice. "I'll see if Stephanie feels like some juice."

Allie slumped down in her chair, growling inside her head. She wished she could be Paul and charm her way into extra privileges. Maybe, by some miracle, she'd be charming when she was seventeen, but that would be a little late for Mighty Mouse and Little Lulu. She growled again.

"What's that about?" her dad asked.

Allie sat up. "Did you hear that?"

"You mean you sounding like an angry dog? I did."

"Oh, sorry, Dad. I was... I was..."

"The faster you eat your breakfast and do your chores, the faster you'll get to the television set."

"Yes, sir."

Allie put syrup on her French toast and glared at Paul out of the corner of her eye. If he wasn't so charming, she'd think about bumping him off and moving up a slot on the favorites ladder.

Chapter Nineteen

It was Monday, and they were standing on Mrs. Hemmett's porch. It was taking a long time for Mrs. Hemmett to open the door, and Allie's basket was getting heavy.

"Maybe she's not home."

Her mother gave her a look. "Of course she's home. She shoveled a path for us."

"Oh yeah." Allie noted the narrow path through the snow that led from the front door, across the porch, and down the steps—just wide enough for two people to walk side by side. Allie shifted the basket again. She knew her mom had given up the idea of doing the laundry herself because she was desperate. She was down to only two dresses that Trudy would tolerate. Allie didn't know what kind of magic soap Mrs. Hemmett had in her laundry room that made such a difference, but it was obvious her mom didn't know the secret.

The door opened. "Afternoon, Mrs. Whitman." Mrs. Hemmett shoved open the screen door and reached for Allie's basket. "Afternoon, Allie."

"Afternoon, Mrs. Hemmett. Thanks for the path," Allie said cheerily.

Mrs. Hemmett grunted and reached for her mom's basket. "You can't pick up on Thursday like usual because it's..."

"Thanksgiving. Yes, I know," her mom said. "Friday?"

"That's fine. How's your boy doing?"

"Fine. He's doing just fine."

Allie wondered why they were talking to each other like strangers at the supermarket.

Her mom turned. "Come on, Allie. You have homework to do."

Allie didn't move. "So, what are you doing for Thanksgiving, Mrs. Hemmett? Want to come to dinner at our house?"

Her mom spun around. "Allie Whitman!"

Allie jumped. "What?"

You can't just invite someone to dinner like that."

"You can't?"

"No."

"Why not? The Sumerian did it?"

"What?"

"The Good Sumerian invited the beat-up guy to dinner." Her mother was staring at her like she'd lost her mind. Allie grunted. "Oh yeah, you missed church because you were home with Tru and Stephanie. Anyway, it was this story Pastor Kline told."

"The Good Samaritan," Mrs. Hemmett offered.

"Yeah, that guy!" She glanced at Mrs. Hemmett and saw a crooked grin on her face, but when she looked back at her mother, it seemed as though *her* face couldn't decide what it wanted to look like. Finally, her mom pressed her lips together and took a deep breath.

"I...I will need to talk with your father first. And did you forget that your sister has the measles? So, I don't think..."

Mrs. Hemmett's crooked grin widened. "It's fine, Mrs. Whitman. I couldn't come anyway." She turned to wink at Allie. "But thanks for asking. I have a meeting to attend with some friends and afterward we have a potluck dinner."

"You have friends?"

"Allie!"

Mrs. Hemmett croaked out one of her laughs. "Yep. A couple."

"Sorry, I didn't mean to be rude, Mrs. Hemmett. Sometimes it just happens."

"I totally understand."

"We need to get home now, Allie."

"Yeah, okay," Allie said turning to go. She hesitated and turned back. "I'm glad you have some place to go for Thanksgiving."

"Thank you, Allie."

Mrs. Hemmett went inside and closed the door. Allie heard the soft *click* of the lock and sighed. Allie had always thought that Horrible Hemmett was locked inside her scary, dirty house, glaring out at the world through grimy windows and eating old crusts of moldy bread, but she wasn't locked in at all. The town never really saw much of her, but she went out. She went out to buy Oreos and magic soap. She went out to buy the stuff to make her mom's special caramel popcorn ball recipe. She went out to find poor animals squished on the side of the road and give them proper burials. She went out to have potluck dinner with her friends.

"Wake up, little miss!" her mom called to her. Allie turned and saw her mom at the car, waving for her to get moving.

"Sorry! I was just..."

"Let's go! Hurry!"

Allie raced down the stairs, concentrating hard so she didn't fall. She didn't want to give her mom another reason to be mad at her. She thought she might have been glad about her invitation to Mrs. Hemmett for Thanksgiving dinner. She thought her mom would say, "Well done, Allie! That's the way to show compassion." But instead it seemed she had made another mess of things. Yep. Obviously, there were rules about inviting people to Thanksgiving dinner—rules that Allie hadn't learned. She figured the list of the things she didn't know or understand was longer than the distance from here to the moon.

Growling at herself, she yanked open the car door and slumped into the seat. Her mom started the engine and pulled out of the driveway. She didn't say anything as they drove along, and Allie was perfectly happy with that arrangement. Her brain was busy thinking about growing up, and how sometimes she liked it and sometimes she didn't.

They came to the cross street and her mom turned left, heading toward the lake.

Allie frowned for a moment, and then she sat forward excitedly. "That's right! I'm going to Sharon's house for sledding!"

Her mom gave her a look. "My goodness, Allie, I think sometimes if your head wasn't attached, it would fall off. *You* packed your snow clothes."

"I know. I forgot for a minute. I was thinking so much about Mrs. Hemmett and Thanksgiving."

"Well, don't forget to call after sledding and your father will pick you up."

"Sledding and dinner," Allie reminded.

"That's right, dinner, too." Her mom shook her head. "Probably hot dogs or something."

"Actually, Sharon's mom is going to make us special German food." Her mom didn't say anything as she turned into the Smiths' driveway. "Look! There's Frances!" Allie said happily. "Are you sure I can't stay a little longer after dinner?"

"No. You know I don't approve of frivolous get-togethers on school nights."

"But it's Sharon's birthday."

"That's why I said yes, but enough is enough. I just can't understand why any mother would plan a party on a school night."

Allie hopped out, opened the back door, and grabbed the paper bag and wrapped birthday gift off the seat. "Okay, Mom. Thanks! I promise to call Dad right after dinner and the cake."

"Wait a minute! Cake?"

Allie slammed the door and hurried to catch up to Frances before she went into the house. She didn't turn around to wave good-bye because she didn't want to see her mother's face. Allie was sure the look would be telling her that she'd broken another rule, and at the moment, Allie was much more interested in friends and sledding than a bunch of do's and don'ts.

* * *

The girls squealed as the toboggan flew over a bump in the track. They tumbled off into the snow laughing and spluttering as the toboggan continued its slide to the flat. Allie sat up, wiping snow out of her eyes and searching for her friends. Sharon was standing and brushing snow off her pants, but Frances was still down, her head buried in a drift.

"Frances!" Allie called out. "Are you all right?" She jumped up and waded as quickly as she could over to her friend. "Frances?"

Frances flipped herself onto her back, laughing hysterically. "My mom would have had a heart attack if she'd seen that."

Allie helped Frances to stand. "And my mom would have been yelling at the top of her lungs, 'Allie Whitman, stop being so reckless; we don't need a doctor's bill for a broken arm!'"

Sharon joined them, laughing. "Moms are weird."

"Yeah, so weird," Allie agreed.

Just then Sharon's mom called from the house. "Come on, kids! Dinner!"

"Wahoo!" Sharon yelled hurrying to climb the hill. "My mom may be weird, but she can really cook *bizarr!*"

"What's that mean?" Allie asked, trudging after her.

"It means 'great' in German," Sharon explained.

On the climb up the hill, they were joined by Jimmy and John Backman, and Todd Fisher. Allie couldn't imagine why Sharon had invited Todd to her birthday party. He was a pest who talked too much, made stupid jokes, and teased everybody. But it was Sharon's party, and she could invite anybody she wanted—all Allie needed to do was stay as far away from him as possible.

"Hurry up, you guys! I'm starving!" Sharon called.

Allie was going to say something about starving kids in China, but by this time they'd reached the top of the hill and something caught her eye that took any words right out of her mouth. She stood there gawking at the house across the street. It wasn't the broken window patched with cardboard, or the mangy cat sitting on the porch that took away her voice and made her squint, but the blue and white car parked in the driveway.

"Sharon!" Allie barked.

Sharon gave her a funny look as she leaned the toboggan by the side door of her house. "What?"

"That...that blue and white car wasn't there before," Allie said, pointing.

"So?"

"Where'd it come from?"

"I guess Mrs. Turner came home from work."

"Turner?"

"Yeah, the Turner family. Well, it's just Mrs. Turner and her son."

Just then Frances came panting to Allie's side. She looked at what Allie was looking at and yelped. "Gopher guts! It's the car!" She punched Allie's arm. "Isn't that the car that your..."

"Yes!" Allie said quickly. "The car from Halloween night."

Sharon gave the car a long look. "That *is* the car. I didn't get a very good look at it that night, but I'm sure you're right." She turned back to Allie. "What's your brother doing riding around with a hoodlum like Mike Turner?"

Allie shook her head. "Being stupid." She decided to change the subject. "So, is anyone else hungry? Because I can't wait to eat bizarre German food."

* * *

As her dad drove her home after the party, Allie knew she should have been happy—the sledding was fun, the dinner of German sausages and mashed potatoes was great, the chocolate cake was yummy, and Sharon loved the Concentration board game Allie had given her. She said it was very sophisticated. So, why did she feel like she'd just gotten a D on a test?

"You okay?"

"Huh?"

Her dad glanced over at her. "Too much cake?"

"No."

"Too much sledding?"

"No."

"Too much..."

"No, Dad. I'm just tired."

He looked at her again, this time for longer. "Okay. I'll just leave you alone."

Allie turned to look out the side window. It was seeing that stupid blue and white car that had ruined everything. And now she had a full name to go with the stupid car. Mike Turner. She wanted to turn to her dad and spill the beans about everything. Her Mom and Dad knew Paul had been drinking Halloween night with some of his buddies, but they didn't know it was the same punk kid Mike in the blue and white car that he'd promised his family never to ride with again. And they didn't know he'd been in that car the day she'd dug up Mr. Stubbs's bones for the science project. And they certainly didn't know that he'd lied about being at Jennifer Green's house the night she almost got run over on her bike. So, if he wasn't at Jennifer Green's house, where was he that he could show up so quickly to help her? If he'd lied about being at Jennifer Green's house, he could have lied about the car from that night. Maybe it wasn't a little old man. Maybe it was the punk kid Mike and his blue and white car—and maybe Paul had been with him. Her brother and his stupid friends had almost run her over! Suddenly the German sausages started a war with the chocolate cake, and her stomach turned over.

"Dad! Stop! Stop the car! I don't feel so good."

"Are you going to vomit?"

"I think so." And then she did—right into the bag of her snow clothes.

Chapter Twenty

"You threw up on your snow clothes?"

"Yep."

"I hope it wasn't my mom's dinner that made you sick," Sharon said, looking apologetic.

"No, it wasn't that. Dinner was really good. My stomach was just upset for some reason."

Frances pushed away her bologna sandwich. "Can you guys stop talking about throw-up and stuff? I can't eat my lunch."

"Sorry, Frances," Allie said, taking a bite of her peanut butter and jelly sandwich. "Let's talk about something else."

Frances brightened. "I'm excited about the Thanksgiving holiday!" she said, retrieving her sandwich. "How about you guys?"

"Of course!" Allie said brightly. "Thanksgiving is the best."

"Yep," Sharon said through a bite of apple.

Frances opened her carton of milk. "We're going to Big Sur to visit my aunt and uncle."

"That'll be fun," Sharon said. "No snow for you." She munched on her apple. "We're staying here, and the Fishers are coming over for dinner."

"What?" both Allie and Frances said together.

Allie was staring. "Todd Fisher? Todd Fisher from our class?"

"Yep. My mom found out that she and his mom are second cousins or something, so now she's decided to take the family under her wing."

"What's that mean?" Frances asked.

"It means Mom wants to look out for them."

"Do they need someone to look out for them?"

Sharon leaned in, and Allie and Frances did, too. "Todd's mother is kinda crazy."

Allie frowned. "What do you mean?"

Sharon leaned in even closer. "Promise not to say anything to anybody about this?" Both Allie and Frances crossed their hearts. "Well, she gets in these bad moods, and then she hits Todd and his brother and sister."

Allie shrugged. "Well, we all get spanked once in a while...or we used to when we were little."

Sharon shook her head. "No. I mean she hits them, and slaps them, and locks them in closets."

"Oh, she doesn't really do that," Frances whimpered.

"She does. I'm not making it up."

"Somebody ought to stop her," Frances said in a timid voice. "Mr. Fisher ought to stop her."

"I heard my mom and dad talking, and they said he was too afraid to stand up to her. So, that's why my mom's inviting them to dinner and stuff like that."

Allie looked around to find Todd. He was sitting with his friend Sam, and they were having a laugh about something. Allie knew she wouldn't be able to laugh about anything if her mom locked her in a closet. She turned to Sharon. "That's why you talk to him."

Sharon nodded.

The end-of-lunch bell rang, and the girls gathered up the remains of their lunches and headed to recess. Allie didn't feel like playing Fox and Geese with the other kids. She sat on the swing and watched as soft flakes of snow disappeared into the drifts. Her brain was busy thinking about a different life. What if she lived Frances's life, as an only child with parents who took care of her every wish—or Sharon's life, full of sisters and world travel—or Todd's life...Todd's life. No, she didn't want to think about living Todd's life. She doubted if Todd's mother had any favorites at all.

* * *

The reenactment of the Pilgrim's first Thanksgiving was a success. The few members of the class who participated as Pilgrims and Indians were taking their bows as the rest of the class clapped. Mr. Nessen was clapping and saying, "Bravo!" So, Allie and Sharon joined him. Their bravos went to Frances, who had played a very believable Pilgrim on the brink of starvation. Even though she'd had a bologna sandwich only a couple of hours earlier, she looked very hungry sitting around the fake campfire with the other religious outcasts.

Sharon sent some of her bravos to Todd who (of course) played an Indian. At one point in the performance, Todd grabbed one of Frances's braids and pretended to chop it off with his cardboard hatchet. Mr. Nessen laughed with the boys, and then gently reprimanded him. Allie would normally have been angry at his behavior and called out a few mean remarks, but today she didn't feel like it. She found herself watching his face and wondering what it looked like when he was locked in the closet. She felt an icy chill run all over her body, and she shook her head, hoping the scary picture would fly out of her ear and into the trash can. Mr. Nessen was walking to the front of the classroom, and Allie was glad for something else to focus on.

"Thank you, Pilgrim presenters! You did a stellar job! Frances, I could almost hear your stomach rumbling with hunger. Now, you actors take off your costume pieces and put them in the bin. I'll sort them later. Quiet as you do so, as I am going to be giving an assignment and I don't want you to miss it." Several of the students groaned, and Mr. Nessen smiled. "You didn't think I'd let your minds go to mush over a four-day holiday, did you?"

"No, Mr. Nessen," they chorused.

"Well, of course not. I care too much for you to allow laziness." He moved to the board and wrote: *The Secret of Thanksgiving.* "Any guesses on your assignment?" No one answered. No one had a clue, not even Charlene Hastings. Mr. Nessen smiled again. "Then the first part of the assignment will be to discover the meaning, after which you are to write a page or two on what that means to you. Any questions?"

"When's it due?" Todd Fisher asked.

"Perhaps in a couple of weeks, but the meaning and an outline will be due the day you get back to school." He gave Todd a wink as the bell rang. "Have a great holiday, my young scholars!"

Allie, Sharon, and Frances met by the cupboard to pick up their lunch boxes and school bags.

"Any idea what the answer to our assignment is?" Sharon asked right away.

Allie shook her head. "Nope."

"Maybe he wants to see if we think Thanksgiving is more than just eating turkey," Frances offered.

"Could be," Sharon answered with a shrug. "But I'm not going to start thinking about it until Sunday night." Her friends laughed with her as they joined the rest of the excited kids in the hallway; everyone was jostling, and talking, and laughing.

The secret of Thanksgiving, Allie pondered as she walked along with her friends. Last Christmas, Pastor Kline had asked the congregation to think about the secret of *Christmas.* Allie couldn't figure that one out, either. The Sunday before Christmas, Pastor Kline told them that the secret of Christmas was Easter. Allie had been totally confused by that. Maybe she'd ask Trudy what she thought about the secret of Thanksgiving. Sometimes her little sister came up with very interesting answers to things.

Chapter Twenty-One

"The fork goes on the left side of the plate on top of the napkin."

"Stop bossing me."

"I'm not bossing you. I'm just telling you proper etiquette."

Allie rolled her eyes at her sister. "I didn't know there was etiquette for silverware," she said testily, but she put the fork on the left side on the napkin. "Anyway, don't talk or you'll infect me with your measles."

"I'm not contagious anymore."

"You still have spots."

"I know, but the doctor told Mom I can't give them to anybody now."

"Then why are you way over there on the couch with a pillow and blanket?"

"Mom didn't want me to miss Thanksgiving, and she thought I'd be more comfortable here than sitting at the table. What's it to you anyway?"

"Well, you're just over there comfortable, and I'm doing all your work."

"Don't you think I'd rather be doing what you're doing instead of sitting here sick?"

Allie didn't have an argument for this. She knew Stephanie loved to help with preparations for parties and holidays: Pilgrim hat napkin holders, harvest-themed centerpieces, and little pine-cone turkey place holders with each person's name written on one of the tail feathers. All that froufrou made Allie's head spin, but Stephanie did it all with flair.

Trudy stood up from her table. "There will not be any snow today."

"Good to know, Tru," Stephanie said.

Trudy moved to Allie and held out her hand. "I will help."

"Really?" Allie questioned, a shocked look on her face.

Trudy returned an innocent face. "Really, what?"

"You want to help?"

"Yes."

"Okay." Allie handed her the rest of the napkins. "Put one on the left side of every plate. Like this one." She pointed to the finished place setting at the head of the table.

"Okay," Trudy answered, taking her time to place the first napkin by the side of the plate. The second napkin unfolded, and she spent several minutes refolding it.

Allie growled. "This is going to take forever!"

"Give her a chance. It's nice that she wants to help," Stephanie said.

"I know," Allie shot back. "It's just that I have to wait for her before I can put on the fork."

"Well, put on the knife and spoon at the rest of the places and then go back for the forks."

"Yeah, okay," Allie said grudgingly, moving to the task.

After a few moments, Stephanie sighed. "It's so plain."

"What?"

"The table."

It was true. It was fun to have the big folding table set up in the living room, but Nana's ivory tablecloth and napkins, and her parents' white embossed wedding china didn't add any color to the table. It was fancy, but not very cheerful.

"Maybe Mom would let us put some pine branches in the center," Allie offered.

"Ugg! That's too Christmassy," Stephanie said, rolling her eyes. She sighed again. "I was going to do this whole big cornucopia, but I just didn't feel up to it."

"What's a cornucopia?"

Stephanie hesitated. "It's...it's like a basket laid on its side with all these harvest things spilling out."

Allie's eyes widened, and she tried not to laugh. "Oh yeah, that sounds really pretty."

"What would you know?"

At that moment the door opened, and Dad entered, escorting a small brown bear into the room. Trudy dropped the napkins and headed back to her table.

"Mom! Dad's here with Mrs. Lawson!" Allie yelled. She heard Stephanie moan from the couch. Mrs. Lawson was not one of Stephanie's favorite people.

Mrs. Whitman came to the kitchen door. "It's not polite to shout, Allie." She moved to Mrs. Lawson and held her cane, as Mr. Whitman removed her fur coat and hat. "Good evening, Mrs. Lawson. We are so glad you could join us for Thanksgiving."

"Hang that in the closet right away now, Alan," Mrs. Lawson instructed briskly. She then turned to Mrs. Whitman with a smile. "Thank you for inviting me, Patricia. It smells good in here."

"Thank you, Betty. The turkey's resting, and I'm just finishing with the potatoes and rolls. Have a seat and I'll bring you a ginger ale."

Mr. Whitman piped up, "I can get it!"

Mrs. Lawson pointed a finger at Allie. "Little miss can get it for me. You've got enough on your hands, Patricia. And Alan, you should help her."

"Yes, absolutely. No problem."

Mrs. Whitman handed her the cane before moving to the kitchen, and Mrs. Lawson set out for Dad's favorite chair. She stopped and fixed Allie with a stare that meant she was not to be challenged. "Well? Don't just stand there like a stump. Ginger ale."

"Oh! Oh, sure. I'd love to get that for you," Allie said, her voice higher than normal. She put down her handful of forks and headed for the kitchen. She was miffed that her mother had scolded her about inviting Mrs. Hemmett to Thanksgiving dinner and yet here was Mrs. Lawson barking orders at everyone and taking over Dad's favorite chair. Of course, she didn't have much of a case against Mrs. Lawson. She had been invited to Thanksgiving for the past four years since her husband, Simon, had died. Her mom and dad knew Mr. and Mrs. Lawson well, having met them in 1945, when they first moved to Lake Tahoe. Paul had been just a baby when they rented one of the cabins at Lawsons' Lodge, and Mrs. Lawson, who didn't have any kids or grandkids nearby, immediately took a shine to the blond-haired baby. Mr. Lawson took a shine to Mr. Whitman, who knew a thing or two about finances and was willing to help him with his taxes.

Allie came back into the front room, placed a coaster on the side table, and set Mrs. Lawson's ginger ale on top.

"Thank you, Allie."

"You're welcome."

Mrs. Lawson leaned forward and looked at Stephanie with that same piercing stare. "Why are you still in your pajamas?"

"I have the measles," Stephanie said. "But I'm not contagious!" she added quickly.

"Nonsense. There's nothing wrong with you," Mrs. Lawson said dismissively, picking up her drink and sitting back. "It's all in your head."

Allie looked over at her sister. *If those spots are all in her head, she has a really great imagination!* She clapped her hand over her mouth so she wouldn't laugh, because Stephanie was staring at Mrs. Lawson as if her hair were on fire.

"But the doctor said..."

"Yes, I know. The doctor said you were sick with the measles. But he does not understand the mathematics and power of the mind when coupled with faith in God."

"So, you've never been sick?" Stephanie asked.

Allie hurried back to set the table, not wanting to be in the center of the argument.

"When I was a girl, I was sick all the time. But when I married Simon, he helped me see the power of faith in God's love."

"Well, I love God, too, Mrs. Lawson, but I still got the measles."

"Maybe sometimes you're sick and you have problems, so you can love God more," Trudy said.

Silence filled the room as the three turned to look at her. Allie was about to say something when her dad came from the kitchen carrying the perfectly browned turkey.

"Happy Thanksgiving!" he said brightly. He set the platter at the head of the table and looked around expectantly. His expression turned to puzzlement as he glanced at the unresponsive faces. "This is not the reaction I expected."

"Oh! Sorry, Dad," Stephanie said quickly. "It's just that Trudy just said something really profound."

Dad smiled. "Well, that doesn't surprise me."

Profound, Allie thought. *That word's going into my diary.*

Mom came in with the potatoes and rolls. "Alright, everyone, time to eat! Allie, would you please bring in the vegetables and the cranberry sauce?"

"Sure." Allie hurriedly set the rest of the forks and headed for the kitchen. When she returned, Mom was placing a tea tray over Stephanie's lap, and Dad was helping Mrs. Lawson to the table. Allie placed the marshmallow yams close to her plate. She sat down and looked expectantly at her dad. *Turkey time!*

"Where's our boy?" Mrs. Lawson asked, settling into her chair.

"Out with friends playing basketball," Mom said, checking her watch. The smile slid off her face. "But he knew dinner was at four and he's late."

"Should we wait for him?" Dad asked.

Allie giggled silently. She could see that her dad was hungry for turkey and stuffing, and waiting was the last thing he wanted to do.

"No. Absolutely not," Mom answered. "He has a watch." She smoothed her dress and sat down. "Alan, perhaps you could say grace before you carve the turkey?"

He sat down and smiled. "Of course, we have many things to be thankful for today." Everyone bowed their heads. "Dear Lord, we thank Thee for this good Thanksgiving Day. We are glad to have Mrs. Lawson with us. We are grateful for our family. We are grateful for this wonderful feast set before us and for Patricia who worked so hard to prepare it. We pray it may be good for our bodies, and that..."

The door opened, and Paul came stumbling into the foyer. The family looked up in surprise.

Mrs. Lawson gained her wits first. "Well, there he is! There's that handsome boy. Only a few minutes late."

Paul focused on the table. "Huh?"

"You're late, son," Dad said.

"Late?"

"For Thanksgiving dinner," Allie said, glaring at him. She still hadn't shared her suspicions about the night of the bike crash, and her anger at her brother bubbled up every time she saw him.

Paul seemed to gather himself. "Oh, yeah, yes, of course. Sorry, Mom. I'm not feeling well." He took off his letterman's jacket and attempted to hang it on one of the foyer hooks. It took him three tries. "I started getting really sick at the end of the game." He headed for the stairs.

"Oh, we are so sorry, dear boy," Mrs. Lawson said.

Stephanie's eyes popped open at this remark. "But don't worry, Paul," she said sweetly. "It's all in your head. You'll be fine in no time."

Paul hesitated. "What? Oh, yeah. I'll be fine. I just need to lie down for a while." He continued toward the stairs. "You guys go ahead without me."

No one said anything as Paul stumbled up the stairs.

Mom stood.

"Where are you going, Patricia?"

"To the kitchen. I forgot the stuffing and gravy."

Allie noted that she moved stiffly, and her lips were pressed together.

Dad took a deep breath and stood also. "Well, amen to the prayer. We *are* very grateful for this day...no matter what happens," he ended on a mumble. He picked up the carving fork and knife. "Now let's eat some turkey!"

"Hoorah!" Allie cheered. With Stephanie on the couch, Trudy at her table, and Paul upstairs sick, Allie was the only kid at the table with the grown-ups. It felt odd—and lonely. She decided she would concentrate on her dinner, and only speak if spoken to. Hopefully Mom would notice and be grateful for her and her good etiquette.

Chapter Twenty-Two

Allie was working on her hand loom, weaving together yellow and orange loops to make a pot holder for her mom's Christmas gift. She was concentrating so hard that she missed the first cry of sirens. When another set was added, she glanced over at Trudy as she began rocking and moaning.

"Mom?" Allie yelled, but her mom was already racing down the stairs.

"My goodness, what a dreadful noise!" She scooped Trudy up in her arms. "Come on, little one. Let's get you to your room."

Mom had nailed thick quilts on all the walls of Trudy's room, so it was the quietest place in the house. When another set of sirens blared into the evening air, Allie felt like joining them for some relief from the racket. She set down her loom and put her hands over her ears. The last time there were this many sirens, the Browns, three blocks over, had lost their summer cabin to a fire. Allie hoped that wasn't the case this time. The smell of smoke had stayed in the air for weeks.

The noise finally subsided, and Allie went back to work on the pot holder. It made her feel grown-up to be in the front room by herself. Dad was at his Rotary meeting, and Paul and Stephanie were off somewhere doing high school stuff. Allie stood up to put another log on the fire, careful to close the fire screen when she was done. She stood in front of the warmth for several minutes, listening for any sound or movement from Trudy's bedroom, but it was quiet. Maybe the two had fallen asleep—Allie smiled at the thought. That meant she truly had the house to herself. What could she do that she normally couldn't with a houseful of family? Her mind finally landed on bread pudding. Should she take a chance and sneak a spoonful of the dessert from the refrigerator? She tiptoed into the kitchen, secured a tablespoon from the drawer, and slowly pulled open the refrigerator door. Just as she was lifting a corner of the Tupperware bowl; the phone rang. Allie jumped, and the spoon clattered to the floor. She snatched it up, threw it back into the drawer, and ran for the phone.

"Hello?" she said in a rush, trying to catch her breath. "Hello?" Oh! Hi, Dad! What's up? Aren't you in your Rotary meeting?" She coiled the phone cord around her finger while she waited for the answer. "Mom? She's in Trudy's room. There were these sirens a little while ago that scared her...not Mom...but Trudy." She paused. "What? Oh, sorry. Sure, I'll go get her." Allie laid the receiver on the table and went to Trudy's room. She knocked several times before her mom opened the door.

"What is it?" she asked in a harsh whisper.

Allie stepped back. "Ah, Dad's on the phone."

"What does he want?"

"I don't know, but he said it was really important."

"Two minutes of rest," her mom mumbled as she softly closed the door and headed for the kitchen.

Allie went back to the front room, picked up her loom, and plopped onto the couch with a growl. She was rankled that she'd missed her chance for extra bread pudding. She leaned forward and eavesdropped on her mom's phone conversation.

"Yes, Alan, what is it?" There was a long pause. "What do you mean, an accident?"

Allie stood up. "Car? Mrs. Hemmett doesn't have a car, Alan." *No, she has an old beat-up truck,* Allie thought. "Hit by a car? I don't understand what you mean?" Allie went to the kitchen door. Mom's voice was loud and irritated. "Then why are you telling me this, Alan, if you don't have all the details?" Her mom listened intently, and then her face drained of color and she sat flat down on the floor. The phone receiver hit the linoleum with a bang, and Allie jumped. She could hear Dad's voice calling from the other end of the line, but her mom didn't move. Allie ran and picked up the receiver.

"Dad, it's Allie! Mom collapsed on the floor. I think she might pass out or something. What do I do?" She looked at her mother's face. "Her eyes are open, but she's just staring. What happened?" Allie started crying. "Okay, okay. I'll try. Get home fast." She hung up the phone, knelt by her mom, and patted her face. "Don't be mad, okay? Dad told me to do this. He's on his way home. He'll be here in a few minutes. He says he called Mrs. Rose. She's coming over." Allie patted her mom's face again a little harder. "Mom, what did Dad tell you?"

Her mom shoved Allie's hands away. "Please, stop that!"

"But Dad said..."

"I don't need my face slapped."

Allie folded her arms across her chest. "Sorry. Are you okay?"

"No, I'm not okay. Mrs. Hemmett was hit by a car."

"What?"

Her mom pushed herself to her feet. "Paul was in the car."

Allie hopped up. "Paul was in what car? Mom, what do you mean?" Allie tugged at the sleeve of her mom's sweater, but she was obviously ignoring her. She was frantically searching around the countertop and in the kitchen drawers.

"Where are my keys? I have to get to Paul. He's hurt."

"Mom! Is Mrs. Hemmett dead?"

"I don't know! I don't know, Allie! Stop asking me questions. I have to get to Paul." She found her keys and grabbed her purse.

Allie clutched at her mom's sweater. "Wait! Wait! Dad's coming home. Wait for Dad!"

"I need to get to the clinic." She bumped into a kitchen chair and knocked it over. "Why the hell don't we have a hospital in this town?"

Allie let go of the sweater. She couldn't move or talk. She'd never heard her mom swear before, so she just stood staring, tears running down her face.

Trudy came howling into the kitchen at that moment. "It's too loud! Too loud!" There was a knock at the door, and Trudy started slapping her head with her hand.

"Allie, go answer the door!" Mom barked as she went to Trudy and grabbed her wrists. "Stop! Stop, Trudy. It's all right."

Allie dragged her sleeve across her eyes as she ran for the front door. She heard her mother's voice trying to calm her younger sister, but it wasn't working. Allie took a deep breath and opened the door. Mrs. Rose was standing there in an overlarge coat and curlers. Allie opened the door wider. "Hi, Mrs. Rose. Come in."

Mrs. Rose stepped into the foyer. "Oh my. Trudy is in a state." Allie took her coat and gave it a strange look. "It's my husband's coat. I was in such a rush I grabbed the wrong coat."

Allie nodded and hung it on a peg. "What did my dad say to you?"

Mrs. Rose set off for the kitchen. "Just that your mom needed me to watch Trudy while they were at the clinic."

"Anything else?" Allie asked, following after her.

"No."

They reached the kitchen.

"Patricia, what can I do?" Mrs. Rose asked immediately.

"See if you can get her to calm down."

"Of course." She grabbed a lap blanket off the back of her dad's chair, moved beside Mrs. Whitman, and wrapped the blanket around Trudy's shoulders securing it tightly in front. "I think the sun is going to shine tomorrow, Miss Trudy," she said in a calm voice. "I think there's only going to be a few wispy clouds way up in the sky. A few wispy clouds. Are those called cirrus?"

Trudy abruptly stopped howling and stared at Mrs. Rose. "No."

"Cumulus?"

"No. Cirro stratus."

"Are you sure?"

"Cirro stratus if they're high. They look like white feathers."

"Ah. Should we go to your room and draw them?"

Trudy turned to her mother. "Should I?"

Allie watched as her mom took a breath and nodded. "I think that would be nice."

The front door opened, and Mr. Whitman came into the foyer.

"Daddy, I'm going to draw," Trudy said.

"Good. That's good, sweetheart. Thank you, Mrs. Rose. I...I don't know when we'll be back."

"Don't worry. I'll be here." The two continued toward Trudy's room.

Allie had never seen her dad so agitated before. His face was chalky white, and the look in his eyes was like he'd forgotten something and couldn't remember what it was. As soon as the bedroom door closed, he took her mother's arm. "Patricia, we have to go—now."

"How is he? How badly is he hurt?"

"I don't know. I don't know, Patricia." He helped her on with her coat. "The ambulance is transporting him."

"How do you know?"

"Sheriff Crandall was at the Rotary meeting when his deputy came in to get him."

"But why was Paul in that car?"

Dad's voice turned harsh. "I don't know, Patricia! Stop asking me questions." He opened the door. "Let's get to the clinic."

"I'm coming, too!" Allie yelled.

"No, Allie. You stay with Mrs. Rose."

"No, Dad!" Allie grabbed at the closing door and pulled hard. "I'm coming, too!" Her voice strangled with tears. "I'm coming with you! I'm coming!"

Mother glared at her, but her dad gave in. "Grab a coat."

Allie yanked the first coat her hand touched as she scrambled after her parents. Her heart hurt, and she was having a hard time breathing. If Paul died, it would be her fault. She was the one who wished him gone so she could move up a step on the favorites ladder. Her *fault*. She tried to silently say a prayer, but it was no use. She knew, without a doubt, that if she tried to sit on that grassy hillside with Jesus, He would tell His apostles to chase her away.

Don't die, Paul. Please don't die. The evening air bit into her skin and she threw on her coat, which wasn't a coat at all, but her lightweight jacket. Allie growled at herself. Couldn't she do anything right?

Chapter Twenty-Three

Allie knew there were three places where ghosts walked around: cemeteries, haunted houses, and hospitals. As she and her parents came through the glass front doors of the Tahoe Medical Clinic, goose bumps popped out all over her body, and she glanced anxiously down the hallway expecting to see shimmery white fog. Maybe she'd see Mrs. Hemmett's ghost wandering around if she was dead. Allie started crying. She didn't want Mrs. Hemmett to be dead. If she was dead, her ghost probably knew that Paul was in the car that hit her. Would he be haunted forever by Mrs. Hemmett and all her ghost animals from the graveyard?

They arrived at the front desk, and her dad said something, and the lady said something, but Allie didn't hear any of it. She was trying to stop her tears and trying to find a tissue because her nose was running. She found an old napkin in her pocket with dried strawberry jam sticking some of the layers of paper together, but luckily there was enough clean area to blow her nose. There wasn't enough to wipe her eyes, though, so she did that on the sleeve of her jacket. She shivered. Stupid lightweight jacket.

Her mom and dad were moving quickly down the hallway, and Allie hurried to catch up with them. She passed by an open door and caught a glimpse of a nurse standing by a bed. She also saw the blur of a red cardigan hanging on a hook and stopped short. Mrs. Hemmett wore a red cardigan.

"Allie, come here," her dad called to her. She sprinted over to him. "We're going to sit for a minute until the doctor can speak to us."

"Okay." She sat next to her mom in the small waiting area. "Where's Paul?"

"In one of the treatment rooms," her dad answered looking to the end of the hall and the double swinging doors. "They just brought him in a little while ago."

"And we don't know what's wrong?"

There was an uncharacteristic irritation in her dad's reply. "No, Allie. We don't know anything. Please stop talking." He handed her his notebook and a pen.

Tears pressed at the back of her eyes. "Okay. Sorry." She sat for several minutes writing down all the big words she could think of from the back of her diary, but she could only remember six, and besides, she couldn't spell them correctly without her diction-ary, so she switched to wandering the hallway and counting the linoleum tiles. She found herself meandering toward the room with the red cardigan. She peeked in. There was Mrs. Hemmett. The hospital bed mattress was tilted up at an angle, so she was sitting, but her head was tilted at an angle and her eyes were closed. The side of her face was bandaged, and her left arm was in a sling. Allie felt the press of tears again.

"And who are you?"

Allie stood straighter and looked up at the nurse's face. "I'm... I'm Allie Whitman."

"Family of the patient?"

"What? Family? No. Oh, no. We're just...we just take our laun-dry to her house." Allie felt a twinge of regret about her answer. "But I know her. Me and my mom know her."

"Well, maybe you'd like to come in and sit by her. She could use some positive energy."

Allie didn't know what "positive energy" was all about, but she thought it might be a chance to say sorry for Paul being in the punk kid Mike's car. She looked back to her parents, but they were deep in conversation and hadn't even noticed that she was missing. She followed the nurse into the room.

Mrs. Hemmett's eyes were closed, and she wasn't moving. Allie stood staring. "Is...is she okay?"

"Just sleeping. You can sit there," the nurse whispered. "I just have a few things to check."

"Is...is she gonna live?" Allie whispered back.

The nurse smiled. "Well, the doctor has a few more tests to run. But we think she'll be fine, sore for a month or two, but she'll be fine."

Allie let out a big breath. "That's good." She sat silently as the nurse checked Mrs. Hemmett's pulse and gave her a shot for something.

"So, that's all she needs from me at the moment. Now it's your turn." She gave Allie a wink and turned to leave.

"Will she wake up?"

"Maybe. Maybe not. We have her sedated...so...but, just go ahead and talk to her. It'll be soothing."

"Really? Oh, okay." *Soothing. That was a good word.* The nurse left, and Allie stared at Mrs. Hemmett and cleared her throat. "The nurse told me it would be okay if I talked to you, but I feel kinda silly talking to a sleeping person." She hesitated. "Anyway, I'm glad the cuts and stuff are on the other side of your face from the stitched-up part. The nurse said your face would be fine, and your arm will be fine, too." She felt sadness rising in her chest. "It was my brother's fault, Mrs. Hemmett. Him and that punk kid Mike. I'm so sorry. I'm sure it was just an accident. I mean they wouldn't try and..." Tears leaked out the corners of her eyes. "Anyway..." She remembered Mrs. Hemmett's saddened face the day Paul went to clean the eggs from her porch. "Mike is the kid who threw eggs at us on Halloween." She took a breath, wiped the tears away with the palms of her hands, and looked around the room. "I hope you had a nice Thanksgiving with your friends. Ours wasn't so great. Paul was sick, and Stephanie had the measles...well, the end of the measles, and Mrs. Lawson kept talking about things in Tahoe that happened a million years ago, like rowing out to the island in Emerald Bay to have tea with Mrs. Knight. The dinner was really good, though. Did you guys have turkey? We had turkey, and stuffing, and yams with marshmallows..."

"Allie?"

Even though her dad's voice was soft, it made her jump. "Dad!"

"What are you doing in here?"

"The nurse said I should come in and talk to Mrs. Hemmett."

"Really?"

Allie stood. "Yeah, something about positive energy."

Mr. Whitman shook his head. "This would never happen in a proper hospital." He motioned to Allie. "Come on. I think it best if you stay by us."

Just then her mother's urgent voice came down the hallway. "Alan? Alan, I need you."

Her dad turned abruptly and headed back to the sitting area. Allie followed. When she came out of Mrs. Hemmett's room, she saw her mom standing face-to-face with the doctor and her dad moving quickly to her side. Allie hurried to join them, standing behind her dad so the doctor wouldn't shoo her away.

"Mr. and Mrs. Whitman, your boy's condition is serious at this stage of the examination, but we don't believe any of the trauma is life-threatening." Mom slumped against Dad's side. "Please, sit down." They did, Mom sitting at the edge of her chair, her hands gripping the chair arms. The doctor continued. "We have him heavily sedated as we continue to assess his injuries. Some of them are serious. When the car rolled, your son must have tried to brace himself with his arms against the dash. His left arm is broken in several places, and then during the roll, his right arm was crushed, and his right thumb was severed." Her mother made a sound Allie had never heard before; it was like a young child screaming and a dog snarling all mixed together. Dad stood and paced back and forth in the small space.

"Oh, dear Lord. How could this happen? How? Severed? No. No, not possible. Lord, how could You let this happen?"

Severed? Allie thought. *Did that mean—cut off?* She burst into tears. Her dad stopped pacing and looked at her, then at his wife. She was weeping uncontrollably. He sat down by her side and put his arm around her. "It's okay, Patricia. It'll be okay. We'll figure this out. Shhh, shhh. Stop now. Patricia, please stop."

"Mrs. Whitman, Paul is going to need you to be strong for him."

At the mention of Paul's name, her mom wailed and stood up. "I failed him! I was supposed to protect him. That was my job!"

Allie heard footsteps coming down the hallway. She turned, expecting to see her sister Stephanie. Instead she saw a middle-aged woman in a maid's uniform. She headed straight for the doctor.

"They told me my boy is being transported? What does that mean?"

The doctor glanced at the Whitmans and quickly ushered the woman over to the side. "Yes, Mrs. Turner. We can't handle your boy's injuries here."

Mrs. Turner pulled away. "Why not?" There was desperation in her voice.

"We don't have the facilities. We're transporting him to the hospital in Carson City."

"What's wrong with him?" she pleaded.

The doctor motioned to the nurse who was hurrying down the hall. "Nurse Beckett, please take Mrs. Turner to the emergency bay." He tried to give her a comforting look. "You can ride in the ambulance with him."

But before Nurse Beckett could take the woman away, Mrs. Whitman pushed herself between them.

"Was it *your* son who caused all of this?"

The woman cowered. "What? I don't... What do you mean?"

Mr. Whitman took hold of his wife's arm. "Patricia, leave it alone."

"Your son did this!" she yelled. "Your son almost killed our son!"

The woman started whimpering. "I don't know...I don't know your son. I don't know what happened."

Nurse Beckett stepped in and took Mrs. Turner's arm. "Come on, let's get you to your boy." They moved down the hall and exited through the double doors.

"Patricia, it's not her fault."

"Isn't it? If she'd raised her boy better..."

"And what about your boy? What about Paul?" Allie yelled. She was standing by her chair, her hands balled into fists, a look of rage on her face. "Paul did some really stupid things and you just ignored it! You think he's an angel. You think he never lies just because he's your favorite. Paul and Trudy are your favorites!"

"Allie Whitman!" her dad snapped.

The doctor stepped forward. "We need to keep our voices down."

"Of course. I'm sorry." Her dad moved over to her. "Allie, calm down."

"Stephanie tried to tell you. She knew stuff about him. And I knew stuff, but I didn't tell you because of Mr. Stubbs. 'Cause I'd dug up Mr. Stubbs for my science project and Paul knew that I did..."

Her dad took her arm. "Allie, you're not making any sense."

Allie pulled away from him. "And I knew that he was going around with Mike, but we promised not to tell on each other. But *they* were the ones that made me crash on my bike. Paul was in the car that ran me off the road! Don't you get it? *They* almost killed me, and now they've hurt Mrs. Hemmett and you stand there yelling at Mrs. Turner like it's all her fault!"

The doctor moved forward again. "Mr. Whitman, you're going to need to take her outside."

"Patricia, I'll take her home, then I'll be back." He put his arm around Allie's shoulder and tried to turn her toward the exit, but she resisted.

"Since I'm the last favorite, it probably wouldn't matter if I died."

"That's enough!" her father growled. He grabbed her jacket by the scruff of her neck and marched her out. Allie struggled to look back and saw her mother slump into a chair. *Good. At least now she knows the truth*, Allie thought bitterly.

Her dad shoved open the glass door, and a blast of cold air hit Allie in the face. She gasped and unclenched her hands. Suddenly one of the words from the back of her diary jumped into her mind. *Consequences.* Allie pulled away from her father's grip. She knew there would be consequences after her outburst, but she didn't care. Now that the truth was out, there'd be consequences for everybody.

Chapter Twenty-Four

The bell rang, and Allie glared at the metal wall unit like it was her worst enemy.

"Miss Whitman, I need you to stay after for a few minutes."

"Yes, Mr. Nessen." She put her hands over her ears and closed her eyes to shut out the clamor of her departing classmates. She felt a hand on her shoulder and looked up to see Frances standing beside her.

"I'll call you later. Maybe you can come over."

"Okay. Maybe. But I might have to go to the hospital."

Frances patted her several times, then moved off to meet Sharon, who gave Allie a sad look and a wave. Allie waved back. When they were gone, she turned to watch Mr. Nessen erase the blackboard and pin a picture of George Washington crossing the Delaware on the bulletin board. The din of departing students subsided, and Allie took a deep breath. She had always liked a mix of activity and quiet, but now she just wanted quiet all the time. *Maybe this is how Trudy feels when there are loud noises, or when people argue.*

Mr. Nessen brought his chair from his desk and sat in front of her. He held a paper in his hand and Allie pressed her lips together. She knew he wasn't going to say, "Well done" about this assignment.

"I'm sorry to hear about Paul's accident, Allie." The gentle tone of his sympathy pulled the tears from her eyes, and she quickly hid her face in her hands. Mr. Nessen placed a tissue between her fingers and continued talking. "This is a very difficult time for your family." She nodded but kept her face covered. "How are your mother and father doing?" Allie shrugged. She looked up and shook her head.

"I don't know," she answered finally. She wiped her eyes and nose. "They're mostly at the clinic."

"Of course. And what is Paul's prognosis?"

"What does that mean?"

"It means how the doctors think things will turn out."

Tears came again, and Mr. Nessen handed her another tissue. "They say his left arm will be okay, but he...he lost his thumb, you know...on his right hand, and his right arm..." She shook her head. "They don't know. He has to go to a special doctor in Reno when he's stronger. He probably won't ever play football again."

"I'm so sorry."

Allie liked how Mr. Nessen didn't say much, but she felt comforted anyway. She blew her nose and took a deep breath. "I'm sorry about the assignment, Mr. Nessen."

He smiled and nodded. "I think we should talk about it."

"Okay," she said quietly.

"Please read what you wrote for the outline," he said, handing her the paper.

"I...I didn't write much, Mr. Nessen. I was upset, and..."

"It's all right, Allie. Go ahead."

She looked at the paper and swallowed. Her throat was dry, and she cleared it several times as she stared at the few words she'd scribbled on the paper. "The Secret of Thanksgiving. I don't know, and I don't care." She handed the paper back to her teacher. "Sorry."

"In this instance, Miss Whitman, there is nothing to be sorry about."

Her head came up. "You mean, I'm not gonna get an F?"

"No, because your answer was honest. Right now, you are living in the middle of the assignment."

"I don't understand."

"Gratitude is going to have a much different meaning for you than it does for the rest of the class, Allie. As you go through the next several weeks, I want you to be aware of what's happening and write down your thoughts and feelings. Do you understand?"

"I think so," she said slowly. But she didn't understand at all. She wasn't happy or thankful for anything. In fact, she was angry at her mom and sad that she was angry at her mom. She didn't care at all about the stupid assignment. It didn't seem very important at the moment. "Is that all, Mr. Nessen?"

He nodded and stood. "Tell your parents I'm thinking of them. And praying for your family."

Allie stood also. "Okay."

"I've had Mrs. Carmichael contact your parents about missing the bus. She said she'd drive you home, so just head for the office."

"Oh, okay. Thanks, Mr. Nessen." Allie moved to pick up her book bag and lunch box. "Mr. Nessen?"

"Yes?"

"Do *you* know the secret of Thanksgiving?"

"Good question, Miss Whitman. I will give the class my answer when the assignment is completed."

Allie nodded and headed off to the school office. On the way, she thought about mashed potatoes and gravy, yam and marshmallow casserole, stuffing and turkey. That's what she'd put on her final paper for this dumb assignment; she'd write about her favorite Thanksgiving foods and why she was grateful for them—and why she was ungrateful for cranberry sauce and green beans.

* * *

Mrs. Carmichael had been instructed by Allie's mom to drop her off at the clinic, and although Allie would much rather have gone home to her room and a book, there was no protesting one of Mom's decisions. Allie had only been at the clinic one other time since the accident and it was boring. Her mom and dad spent all their time in the room with Paul, while she and Stephanie sat in the waiting area doing nothing. Well, Stephanie read one of the magazines from the side table, and *Allie* did nothing. She had wanted to go wandering and maybe even sneak in to see Mrs. Hemmett, but Stephanie had told her to "stay put."

So, this visit, because Stephanie was at home watching Trudy, Allie sat by herself in the waiting area, playing with Silly Putty and being bored. She looked down the hall to Mrs. Hemmett's room and saw two women and a man exiting. Allie sat up. *That means Mrs. Hemmett is awake!* Allie stood, shoved the Silly Putty in its egg, and tiptoed over to the closed door of Paul's room. She pressed her ear against it and heard mumbled voices. She prayed they would keep talking for a while, as she crept to Mrs. Hemmett's room. The door was partially open, but she knocked anyway.

"Yes?" Mrs. Hemmett said, a note of curiosity in her voice.

Allie pushed open the door. "Hi, Mrs. Hemmett, it's Allie Whitman. Can I come in?"

"Of course. Don't you know there's no privacy in a hospital." Allie stayed by the door. "You here to see your brother?"

"Mom and Dad are with him. I just wait and twiddle my thumbs."

"That's not much fun."

"No," Allie said, taking one step into the room and stopping.

"Well, don't stand there like a stick. Come on over."

Allie moved to the end of the bed. "Were those your friends I saw leaving?"

"Yep. A few of them from Al-Anon."

"What's Al-Anon?"

"It's a group for people who have alcoholics in their family."

"Alcoholics?"

"Like your brother."

"What? My brother's an alcoholic?"

"Pretty sure."

"Why do you think that?"

"'Cause he's putting everything at risk, and he can't stop himself."

Allie pulled a chair close to the bed and sat down. "From drinking beer?"

"From drinking anything. Beer's probably the easiest thing for his friend to get hold of."

"You mean Mike."

"Is that his name? The one who drives around in that blue and white car?"

Allie nodded. "Mike Turner."

"Made you crash your bike in my yard."

"I know. Paul said it was some little old man."

"Well, alcoholics are really good at telling lies. And, see, even after that scare, Paul didn't stop drinking, did he?" She shifted to a more comfortable position. "I'm not used to being in bed so much. I like to keep busy."

"Sorry you got hurt, Mrs. Hemmett."

"Yeah, me, too. Just trying to get a dead cat off the side of the road, and they came swerving around the corner and hit me. *Bam!*" Allie jumped. "Luckily it was just the side of the car that bumped me, or we wouldn't be having this conversation."

"Sorry."

"Don't worry, I'm tough. Just scraped up a bit, bruised ribs, dislocated shoulder."

"Ow."

Mrs. Hemmett croaked out a chuckle. "Yeah, ow."

"But they didn't mean to hit you, right?"

"What do you mean?"

"They didn't do it on purpose."

Mrs. Hemmett studied Allie's face. "I imagine not. Alcoholics drink on purpose, but what comes after they usually don't know or remember."

"You understand a lot about alcoholics."

Mrs. Hemmett took a deep breath. "Sad to say."

"How come?"

"My husband, Arlo, was an alcoholic."

Allie stared at her, tears welling up in her eyes. "That accident...your accident... He crashed the car, didn't he? He caused the accident that killed..." Allie couldn't go on. Her heart was beating fast, like she was in the car headed for the tree.

Mrs. Hemmett nodded slowly. "He was drunk and..." She winced with pain and it took her a moment to continue. "He shouldn't have been driving."

Tears slid down Allie's cheeks. "How can we make Paul stop drinking?"

Mrs. Hemmett laid her hand on top of Allie's. "You can't *make* him do anything, Allie. The day Paul came over to clean up the eggs, I tried to warn him. Invited him to come with me to AA. Told him about Arlo and the grief he caused, but he didn't want to hear any of it."

Allie absently wiped her face on Mrs. Hemmett's hospital sheet. "I know! He said you were crazy and that we shouldn't see you anymore."

"Doesn't surprise me."

"And Mom believed him."

"Doesn't surprise me, either. She doesn't want to accept what's happening."

Allie stood up abruptly and walked over to the window. "I know! She always takes his side. She always ignores the bad stuff he does. I never get away with anything." Allie turned back and found Mrs. Hemmett frowning at her and felt childish about her outburst. "Well, she does ignore a lot of stuff that he does. Why does she do that?"

"Sometimes it's too painful to look at the truth. But at some point she and your dad are going to have to face the truth and lay down some rules, or Paul might not make it."

"What?"

"It's a sickness, Allie, and it only gets worse."

Allie's stomach hurt. She came back to the bed and sat down. "But there has to be a way to make him stop, Mrs. Hemmett! There has to be!"

"There is a way, but Paul has to choose it."

Mr. Whitman stepped into the doorway. "Allie?" Allie closed her mouth on the next words she was going to say. "You shouldn't be in here bothering Mrs. Hemmett."

"No bother at all. She was keeping me company."

"Well, your mother's been looking for you. I'm surprised you haven't seen her."

Allie stood. "She didn't come in here."

Mr. Whitman cleared his throat. "Sorry about the accident, Mabel. Are you doing all right?"

"Well, it's not like being on holiday in Hawaii."

Allie looked at her dad, and it seemed that Mrs. Hemmett's answer made him uncomfortable.

"Ah, well, no...no, I'd imagine not," he stammered. He held out his hand. "Come on, Allie. Let's find your mother. We need to get home for dinner."

Allie moved to her father, but she didn't take his hand. She stopped at the door on their way out and turned to Mrs. Hemmett. "I'll think of something to do about Paul, Mrs. Hemmett. I know I can."

"You let me know how that works out."

Allie waved and headed after her father. She didn't see Mrs. Hemmett shake her head or hear her sigh.

Chapter Twenty-Five

"'Ye have heard that it hath been said, Thou shalt love thy neighbor and hate thine enemy. But I say unto you, Love your enemies, bless them that curse you, do good to them that hate you, and pray for them which despitefully use you, and persecute you; That ye may be the children of your Father which is in heaven: for he maketh his sun to rise on the evil and on the good, and sendeth rain on the just and on the unjust'" (Matt 5:43-45 KJV).

Pastor Kline laid the Bible on the pulpit and looked out at his congregation. As he continued his sermon on the just and unjust, Allie squinted up at the baby Jesus in the stained-glass window, trying to understand what made Him tick. Love your enemies? What good did that do? They'd probably hate your guts no matter what you did. And what did *despitefully* mean? She'd have to look it up in her dictionary. It sounded like a mean word, and yet Jesus wanted her to pray for the people who despitefully used you? Allie shook her head. She looked over at her mom, who had her head bowed. Maybe she was saying a prayer for somebody. *Maybe she's saying a prayer about me!* Allie thought suddenly. *Maybe she hates my guts because of what I said at the hospital, and now she's praying to find out which scary old aunt to send me to live with until I graduate from high school.*

"So, are there only friendly neighbors or terrible enemies in our lives?" Pastor Kline asked. "What about all the people in between? Are there not casual acquaintances? People that we see every day and yet don't know? How about the neighbor whom everyone talks about? What about the supposed town bad boy or the children in our own families who have gone astray?"

Allie's head jerked up at that statement. She was sure Pastor Kline would be staring directly at her, his pastor spirit somehow knowing about her outburst at the hospital, or the pack of lies she'd been lugging around, or how she had made a dinosaur out of the bones of Mr. Stubbs.

"If we are to love and pray for our friends and our enemies," Pastor Kline continued, "perhaps God is telling us to pray for everyone in between, too. Perhaps He is telling us that *all* of His children deserve our love and prayers."

Allie looked over at her mom. There was only Trudy and Stephanie between them, because Dad had volunteered to stay with Paul, who was now recuperating at home. Mom was wearing Allie's favorite outfit: her brown tweed suit, brown leather shoes and handbag, and black pillbox hat. She looked both elegant and sad. She still had her head bowed, and Allie thought she saw a couple of tears drip onto her folded hands. Allie stood, pushed her way in front of her sisters, and wedged herself into the space beside her mom. Stephanie raised her eyebrows, but Trudy slid sideways to make room.

Mom reached over and laid her hand on Allie's, which caused Allie to start crying like a baby: loud, noisy blubbering that made the congregation turn from Pastor Kline to stare at her. Her mom put an arm around her, lifted her off her seat, and walked with her down the aisle and out into the foyer.

Once the heavy chapel doors closed behind them, Allie knew the congregation had been saved from her caterwauling. She took deep gulps of air and tried to stop the mewling sounds that were tumbling out of her mouth.

"Stupid...sorry...stupid tears. I'm sorry, Mom. Sorry. Please don't send me away to live with Aunt Evelyn!"

Her mom walked into the women's bathroom and returned a minute later with a damp paper towel. She took Allie to the steps that led to the pastor's office. "Sit." Allie sat, and her mom sat beside her, placing the cold folded paper towel on the back of her daughter's neck. Allie shuddered and stopped blubbering.

"Better?" Allie nodded. Mom handed her a tissue. "Good."

They sat in silence as Allie continued to calm down. A brewing storm caused the front doors of the church to rattle, and Allie thought it might be wonderful to be snowed in at home without the noise and bustle of school to worry about. But that meant that her family would be snowed in at home with her, and right now, the family didn't seem to like each other much.

"Mom?"

"Yes?"

"I'm sorry for despitefully using Trudy by digging up her hamster." Her mother was silent. "And I'm sorry for despitefully using you and Dad by lying for Paul." Again, her mother didn't respond. "And..." Allie began to sniffle. "And...I'm sorry for all the mean things I said at the hospital. That was the worst despiteful thing." Her mother handed her a tissue, sitting quietly for several moments.

"I don't have favorites, you know."

Allie sat up and stared at her. "What?"

"I don't have favorites."

"Yes, you do," Allie replied quietly.

"Why do you think that?"

"Well, you spend lots of time with Trudy."

"You know why that is," her mother said in a calm voice.

Allie nodded. "Yeah, I know, but your voice is always soft when you talk to her."

"I see."

Allie was encouraged because her mom was letting her talk— so she went on. "You always smile at Paul and kid around with him about stuff, and you're always talking with Stephanie about her school activities. But with me...you never do anything with me except go to Mrs. Hemmett's house." She broke off because she could feel tears pressing behind her eyes, and she didn't want to start blubbering again.

Her mom turned to her. "Allie, look at me." Allie did, and her mom looked right into her eyes. "Do you know why I talk to Stephanie about school and her accomplishments?"

"Because you like her better."

Her mom shook her head. "No. I do it to distract her from her vanity."

"What's that mean?"

"To stop her worrying about her body, and her face, and her hair."

"Oh yeah, she worries about that a lot."

"She does."

Allie looked down and scowled at the scuff marks on her shoes. "But what about Paul? After Dad and Trudy, he's your favorite."

"Remember, I don't have favorites. I care for each of you differently because you each have different strengths and weaknesses." She let out a sigh that sounded tired—like she'd never had even two minutes of rest, and when she continued speaking, her voice was full of soft sadness. "Paul is the one I worry about the most. I kid around with him to help keep him positive. He's unsure of himself and needs my encouragement."

Allie's mouth dropped open, and she turned to her mother in shock. "What? Paul is not unsure of himself. He's popular. He's on the football team. He's dating that Jennifer girl."

"He's my son, Allie, and I know him." She took a deep breath. "All that outward charm is just a coverup."

"For what?"

"For his insecurity. Paul is very much like my father, and my father never thought he was good enough for anything."

"Grandpa Harrison? But he did a lot of stuff."

"He did. He was in the army, he got married and had a family, he owned a business, but...he...he never felt like he measured up." Allie watched as a tear rolled down her mother's cheek. She moved an inch closer as her mother brushed the tear away with her fingertips. "He could never get control of his drinking."

"Grandpa Harrison drank a lot?" Her mother nodded. "I didn't know that."

"Of course not. Alcoholics are very good at keeping secrets—and telling lies."

"That's what Mrs. Hemmett said!"

"I know."

"How do you know she said that?"

"Because. I was standing outside her room at the hospital, listening to your conversation."

Allie was mortified that her mom had heard her talking behind her family's back. "But...but Dad didn't see you," she stammered.

"I'd probably gone out to the car by that time."

"Oh." Allie felt like the storm outside the church was swirling around in her stomach. "So...you didn't hear what Mrs. Hemmett said about Paul being in danger?"

Her mom shook her head. "No, but I understand why she would say it."

"You do?"

"Of course. My dad was always in danger...always." Another tear rolled down her cheek.

"If you knew Paul was in danger, then why didn't you do something about it?"

"My mother trained us kids to ignore my father's drinking, or minimize it, or lie about it."

Allie gave her a puzzled look. "Well, that doesn't sound good. Let's not do that with Paul."

"There's not an easy solution, Allie."

"Well, we can't just ignore it, Mom! Make him talk to Mrs. Hemmett or go to that AA place. We have to do something! I'm just a kid! I don't know what we should do! I'm not the mom, you are. You're supposed to figure this stuff out!" She began crying. "You're supposed to help us, and do fun stuff with us, and hug us."

Her mother started to stand. "I'll get another cool towel."

"I don't want that! That's not what I need!"

Her mom stared at her for a moment, then sat down close and put her arm around her shoulder. Allie crumpled into her lap.

"I'm sorry I say stupid things, and I lie, and I don't have compassion," Allie sobbed.

Her mom handed her a tissue. "Allie, listen to me. Are you listening?" Allie nodded. "I was wrong, and I owe you an apology."

"What?" Allie hiccupped.

"I haven't been a very good mom to you this year. I'm sorry. I've been very worried about Trudy, and Stephanie, and Paul, and somehow you got left out."

"Except for my lessons on compassion."

Her mom rubbed her back. "I was wrong about that, too. I shouldn't have forced you into that situation."

Allie sat up, and her mom tucked her hair behind her ears and handed her a clean tissue. "No, Mom, you were right about taking me there. I'm glad we went to Mrs. Hemmett's house. She's not scary anymore."

"Well, you have a kind heart, and you would have grown into compassion on your own."

Did Mom just say I have a kind heart? Allie saw herself as the one who wanted to avoid anything disagreeable. Then she realized there'd been some changes; she did care about stuff now. She cared about her friend Frances wanting brothers and sisters, about Todd Fisher wishing his mom was a better mom, about Mrs. Turner's worry for her hoodlum son, about her sister Trudy. Her heart cared about all that stuff. Allie blew her nose and shrugged. "I guess so."

"I know so," her mom whispered. She took Allie's hands. "Now, I'm not a demonstrative person…"

"What's that mean?"

"It means I wasn't raised with much affection and hugging, so I forget that other people might need a hug every now and then." She gave Allie's hands a little squeeze. "But I want you to know that your dad and I love you."

Allie couldn't find her voice in all the emotion, so she just nodded.

"And I'll try and do better about the hugs."

"Okay," Allie sniffed. She started to say something else about hugs, but the music for the benediction hymn started, and both Allie and her mom jumped. Allie brushed away the last of her tears. "Mom, I don't want to be here when all the people come out."

"Me, either!"

So it was that after the majority of the congregation had departed, Stephanie and Trudy discovered their missing mom and sister quietly giggling together in a stall in the women's bathroom of the Presbyterian Church.

Chapter Twenty-Six

All eyes were on Mr. Nessen as he stood from his desk and picked up the black binder. Reading from the Black Binder of Great Thinkers was a cherished tradition in Mr. Nessen's class, as it held sayings from Aristotle, Thomas Jefferson, Helen Keller, Booker T. Washington, Albert Einstein, and Jesus, to name a few. Periodically their teacher would add a quote from some other great thinker and share it with his class for discussion. Today was obviously one of those days, and Allie was excited to "stretch her brain," as Mr. Nessen called it. He brought the high stool to the front of the class, set it down, and held the binder high in the air.

"Good morning, scholars! And what do I hold in my hands?"

"The Black Binder of Great Thinkers!" the class chorused.

"It is, indeed!" He set it on the stool. "But before we get to the reading, I have some announcements to make. First, we are a week away from Christmas..." The class cheered. "Yes, I thought that might get your blood pumping. And that means we are three days away from Christmas vacation!" The class cheered again, and Mr. Nessen joined them. "But, that being said, we still have important work to do in those three days, and I don't want to see anyone's mind wandering. Is that understood?"

"Yes, Mr. Nessen," they all said with smiles in their voices.

"Good. Second, thank you all for turning in your assignments on the Secret of Thanksgiving." He gave Allie a little nod and she smiled. "They were all well done and thoughtful, but I found one sufficiently insightful enough to be included in the black binder." He picked up the book.

Many of the students gasped and several said, "Wow." Everyone sat a little straighter in their seats, and Allie and Frances shared a quick wide-eyed glance.

Their teacher sat on the stool, opened the book, and looked out over his students. "Is everyone attentive?" The class nodded, and he began reading. "'I think the Secret of Thanksgiving is not waiting around for the big things to be thankful for, because a lot of time the big things don't happen. Lots of money. A new car. A perfect family. The secret is to be thankful every day for the little things—like getting this assignment done...'" Mr. Nessen smiled as the class laughed. He shook his head good-naturedly and went back to reading. "'...like getting this assignment done, or sledding with friends, or having waffles for breakfast, or having a new person like you. Sometimes things can be really terrible, and you can't imagine there's one thing to be thankful for, but then you have to remember the secret and you'll find something: new white snow on the ground, a friend that tells stupid jokes, finding a surprise piece of candy in your pocket. Sometimes it can be as small as someone smiling at you. Anyway, that's what I think the secret of thanksgiving is. I've tried doing this every day since getting the assignment, and it works.'"

Mr. Nessen shut the black binder, and after a stunned pause, the whole class clapped, each person looking around to see which classmate might be the "great thinker," but since everyone was clapping, it was impossible to tell.

"That, my dear students, is a very good definition of the Secret of Thanksgiving. Several of you had similar ideas to this, and I applaud your deep thinking." The end-of-school bell rang, and the students started gathering their things and chatting about the paper and who might have written it. Mr. Nessen spoke above the ruckus. "Remember...remember..." The class quieted. "Tomorrow we are making Christmas cards for the elderly, so don't forget your scissors and colored construction paper." The commotion started up again as Allie headed back to the cupboards to gather her book bag and lunch box.

Frances met her as she opened the door. "Wow! Good for you, Allie," she whispered excitedly.

"What?"

"Your thoughts in there with the other great thinkers. It was really a good paper."

"It wasn't me."

Frances gave her a skeptical look. "Come on; you told me you were going to write something about being thankful for the little things."

"Yeah, and I did, but mine wasn't the one he read." She took her book bag off the hook and shoved a few books inside. She smiled. "I guess I was one of the *other* 'deep thinkers.'"

"Then who was the writer?"

Allie shrugged. "Not a clue." She and Frances put on their coats and headed for the door. They passed by Sharon and Todd Fisher, who were having a conversation about something, and Allie heard Sharon say, "It was really good," and she saw Todd look down at his shoes.

Allie stopped short. T*odd Fisher wrote the "great thinker" paper*, she thought.

Frances turned back to her. "What? Why'd you stop?"

"Hang on a minute," Allie said as she moved in Sharon's direction. "I have to ask Sharon a question."

"Well, hurry up or we'll miss the bus."

Allie came up beside Sharon, and she and Todd immediately stopped talking. "Hi, Sharon! Hi, Todd!" She didn't wait for them to respond. "Todd, did you write that paper?"

"Huh?"

"The 'great thinkers' paper. Did you write it?" Out of the corner of her eye, she saw Sharon smile. "You did, didn't you?"

"It's no big deal."

"It is a big deal, and I liked it. Everybody liked it. Well done!"

Todd stared at her for a few moments, then grinned and shrugged. "Thanks."

"Come on, Allie! The bus is gonna leave us," Frances called.

Allie called back to her. "Okay! I'm coming!" She smiled at Sharon and Todd. "See you guys tomorrow."

"Don't forget your scissors!" Sharon called after her as she and Frances ran for the bus.

"What was all that about?" Frances asked in a breathy voice.

"When we're on the bus, I'll tell you a real cool secret," Allie said. She felt like skipping the rest of the way to the bus, but that would have been very fourth grade.

Chapter Twenty-Seven

Christmas Eve Day fell on a Sunday, and the pews in the Presbyterian Church were all packed. Allie sat on her mom's left side with Trudy on her right, then Dad, and then Stephanie. Paul was at home continuing to recuperate. Allie was glad his skin didn't look like yellow wax anymore, and that the special doctor in Reno was able to save a part of his thumb, so that maybe, someday, he could hold a pencil. Allie looked over at her dad and sighed. He had said he wasn't coming to church because he was still mad at God for allowing the accident, but when Mom reminded him again that Paul could have died, he put on his Sunday suit and joined the family.

It was a beautiful Christmas Eve Day with fresh snow on the ground and a bright blue sky. Allie was having a hard time containing her excitement for all the happenings that would fill the day. After church she was going sledding with Sharon and Frances at Sharon's house, and then home to a yummy Christmas Eve dinner. Their family's tradition was to have their big dinner the night before Christmas, so Mom could relax on Christmas Day while everybody ate leftovers. The evening would end with setting up the manger scene, and then each family member would open one Christmas gift. Allie had already picked out the one she wanted to open—a small rectangular box with red and green plaid wrapping paper. Allie was hoping it was a watch. She'd wanted a watch since she was eight. Allie heard Pastor Kline say something about Christmas, so she pushed thoughts of sledding and presents to the back of her mind and focused on the pulpit. Pastor Kline was preaching again this year about how Easter was the secret of Christmas, and Allie felt a little shiver of understanding. If Jesus hadn't taught important lessons and paid the price for everybody's sins, then nobody would even care that He was born—well, maybe the shepherds who were told about His birth by angels, but even they would have been kinda mad if Jesus had just given up His special life and gone off to be a carpenter.

Allie looked up to the stained-glass picture of Mary and the baby Jesus. She wished the perfect baby a happy birthday and felt a smile creep onto her lips. She glanced around to see if anybody else was smiling, when something caught her eye. There in the shadow of one of the pillars she could just make out the form of Mrs. Turner. She was hunched into her coat, and it seemed like she didn't want anyone to see her. Allie turned to tell her mother who she saw and then thought better of it. She didn't want her mom yelling at Mrs. Turner on Christmas Eve Day during Sunday service.

The benediction hymn was sung, the prayer was given, and the congregants began filing out. Allie headed down the aisle with the others, but when she turned back, she noticed that her mom wasn't following. In fact, she was headed directly toward Mrs. Turner, and the rest of the family was with her. Allie turned abruptly. *Oh, no! Please not a scene in the chapel.* When she got to her father's side, Allie saw that Mrs. Turner was sitting pressed against the pew, a look of shock on her face. It looked to Allie like she hadn't slept or eaten for days. Mom sat down next to her, and Mrs. Turner scooted back.

"I'm not going yell at you, Mrs. Turner, I promise. What is your first name?"

Allie noticed how her mom was using the voice she used with Trudy when she was trying to calm her.

Mrs. Turner swallowed. "Ruth."

"Ruth, I'm Patricia Whitman, and I apologize for the way I treated you at the hospital. We were both suffering that night, and I was horrible to you. I'm so sorry."

"I... I..."

"How is your son doing?"

At these words, Mrs. Turner fell apart. She put her hands over her face and sobbed. Stephanie put her arm around Trudy's shoulder and led her out to the foyer as Pastor Kline and his wife, Lois, came over to the group. The pastor sat on Mrs. Turner's other side, while Lois knelt in front of her and handed her a handkerchief.

"How can we help?" Pastor Kline asked.

"He's...he's still in Carson. My boy, Mike. He's never going to walk again, Pastor. That's what the doctors say."

Allie looked at her mom as the color drained from her face. "Oh, Ruth...I'm so sorry," her mom whispered.

"I don't even have any way to get down to see him."

Pastor Kline took her hand. "What is your name?"

"Ruth Turner."

"Do you have family?" She shook her head. "Then, here's what I think, Ruth. I think you should come home with me and my wife, Lois, and have a little rest at our house."

"But, Pastor... I...I'm not a member of your church. I just came in because it's Christmas."

"Well, that's a very good reason." He patted her hand. "You rest a little with us, and then tomorrow we'll find a way to get you down to see your boy."

She stared at him. "You will?"

"We will." He looked at the Whitman family. "I think we have this, Alan. Why don't you take your family home?"

"Is there anything we can do?"

"I think we'll be fine, but I'll let you know." He helped Mrs. Turner up from the seat, and his wife put an arm around her waist.

Mrs. Whitman stood and put a hand on Mrs. Turner's arm. "Ruth, I really am so sorry about your son. So sorry."

Mrs. Turner nodded weakly as Lois Kline led her away.

Pastor Kline looked at her mom. "You've started some healing here today, Patricia. It will be a balm as the weeks go on. Have a good Christmas." He turned and moved after his wife.

"Come on, Patricia. Let's get home to check on Paul."

Her mom nodded, and they headed to the foyer. Suddenly she stopped and brought Allie to her side, holding her hand as they continued on.

* * *

The Whitman family was standing on Mrs. Hemmett's front porch—even Paul, with both of his arms in casts. He was breathing hard to keep down the pain, but Allie knew this time he wasn't forced to come; this time he wanted to be on Mrs. Hemmett's front porch. There had been a slight debate among the family about singing a Christmas carol, but they'd decided against it, as none of them had great voices without the church organ. They knocked instead.

"Who is it?" came Mrs. Hemmett's voice from the other side of the door.

"It's the Whitman family," Mr. Whitman said.

Allie heard the lock turning, and slowly the door opened so that a slice of warm yellow light poured out onto them and the surrounding snow. "What in blue blazes are you doing out on Christmas Eve?"

"We've come to visit!" Allie called from the back of the group.

"Well, my goodness." Mrs. Hemmett shook her head and opened the door. "Well, come in. Come in. I don't have much to offer you." Her arm was still in the sling, and she moved slowly like every inch of her body hurt.

Stephanie opened the screen door and the family piled in. "That's all right, Mrs. Hemmett," Allie said as she passed by her. "We didn't come empty-handed. We brought you a plate of Christmas dinner, and berry cobbler for dessert!"

"We're sorry to just barge in, Mabel, but it was Paul's idea to come tonight," her mom explained.

Mrs. Hemmett looked puzzled. "Paul's idea?" She studied him carefully. "I'm surprised to see you up and about, young man."

"I'm tough, Mrs. Hemmett. Just like somebody else."

She croaked out one of her laughs. "Well, where are my manners? Everybody sit down. Alan, you can put that cobbler on the table in the dining room and bring some chairs. Allie, you can put that plate of food in the fridge."

"Okay," Allie said moving off to the kitchen.

Mrs. Hemmett nodded at Stephanie and leaned a little to the side to see Trudy, who was hiding behind her mother's back. "Now, these are your girls I haven't met?"

"Yes," Mrs. Whitman said. "This is Stephanie."

"Merry Christmas, Mrs. Hemmett."

"Merry Christmas, Stephanie."

"And this is Trudy," Mrs. Whitman said in a soft tone. "Trudy, Mrs. Hemmett is the lady who washes your dresses."

"So they're not crunchy," Trudy said.

Allie heard this remark as she returned from the kitchen. She wanted to laugh, but she didn't because she knew it would make Trudy feel bad, especially when she was in a new place. "That's right, Tru, no more crunchy dresses," Allie said softly.

"Like Mom did," Trudy said.

Mrs. Hemmett croaked out several laughs, and to everyone's surprise, Trudy peeked around her mom's back and smiled. She ran her hands over the soft fabric of her dress. "Thank you, Mrs. Hemmett."

"You are very welcome, Trudy."

"And we brought a present for you!" Trudy announced suddenly.

"For me?"

"Yes."

"Trudy, why don't we sit down now and let Paul give Mrs. Hemmett her gift, since it was his idea."

Allie noticed that her mom was using her most gentle voice as she led Trudy to the chair.

Paul stood and nodded at Stephanie, who pulled a wrapped gift out of the bag she'd been carrying. She handed it to Mrs. Hemmett and sat down.

Allie watched as Paul tried to compose himself. Finally, he pressed his lips together, took a deep breath, and started. "I'm sorry about the accident, Mrs. Hemmett. Mike and I had been drinking, and we...we didn't know what we were doing. We came around that corner, and we didn't see you. We didn't see you. I swear, it wasn't on purpose."

Allie looked over and saw her mom watching Mrs. Hemmett intently.

"I believe you, Paul," she said simply. "Arlo didn't mean to kill himself and our son, either, but that's what the drink does." Paul flinched, but Mrs. Hemmett went on. "You're gonna have to decide what you want, Paul. Your parents can set some rules, but you're the one to decide. You know what I'm talking about." Paul nodded, and she studied his face for several moments. "Well, okay then, I accept your apology." Paul took a deep breath as Mrs. Hemmett laid a hand on his shoulder. "Now, who wants cobbler?"

Allie's hand shot into the air, and everyone laughed.

The next hour was spent eating berry cobbler and talking about school and life in Tahoe in general. Allie was surprised to find out that Mrs. Hemmett wrote in a journal almost every day, and that Yellowstone National Park was her favorite. It was Allie's favorite, too, although she'd never been there. *Someday,* Mrs. Hemmett told her.

The highlight of their time together was when Mrs. Hemmett opened the gift from Paul and the family to find a dozen Chinese wind chimes. The note inside said:

Something for your animal cemetery.
My aunt and uncle picked them up for us in San
Francisco's Chinatown.
Merry Christmas.
Paul and the Whitman family

She'd flipped the card over and chuckled about the note Allie had added:

I'd still like you to teach me how to make wind
chimes when you feel better.
With admiration,
Allie

Mrs. Hemmett had agreed that it would be great for Allie to carry on the tradition of making wind chimes for the animal cemetery, and she promised to begin the instruction after the New Year.

Allie was excited by the prospect, but she vowed that wind chimes was the limit; she would not be learning how to scoop dead animals off the side of the road.

Chapter Twenty-Eight

"**A**llie! Lights-out in half an hour."

Allie jumped up and raced to open her bedroom door. She poked her head out. "Okay, Mom!" she called down. "We're just about finished!"

"Do you girls need anything?"

"Chocolate chip cookies?" Allie asked hopefully.

"Sorry, Paul took the rest to share at his AA meeting. How about some bananas?"

"Ah, no, thank you." Allie giggled, looking back at her friends and rolling her eyes. "We're fine."

"All right. Have fun."

Allie closed the door and moved to sit on the floor with Frances and Sharon. "Moms are so weird," she said, smiling. *Weird, but necessary*, she thought. She picked up her scissors and the folded piece of red construction paper.

"Who's that big Valentine for?" Sharon asked, gluing a white paper doily onto a pink heart.

"Mrs. Hemmett."

"Oh! I want to make her one, too!" Frances said. "Her caramel popcorn balls are so yummy."

"Maybe she'll make you some for Valentine's Day," Sharon said.

"Do you think so?"

Allie and Sharon laughed at the excitement in Frances's voice.

"Why not?" Allie said. "We could all sign the one I'm doing, and maybe she'll make treats for all of us."

"Deal," Frances said, saluting.

"I'm in," Sharon added. "As long as you guys will sign this valentine I'm making."

"Who's it to?" Allie asked.

"Todd Fisher."

"Of course," Allie answered immediately.

"Not me," Frances said, making a face.

"Why not?" Sharon asked, a bit offended.

"Well, look at that thing!" Frances scoffed. "All pink and lacy and girly. Todd would take one look at that and throw it in the trash."

Allie started giggling. "She's right, ya know. I think we should make him one with scary stuff."

Sharon brightened. "That's a great idea! He'd like that." She pulled a piece of brown construction paper out of the stack, and the three friends went to work covering the paper with black drawings of skulls, ghosts, and hearts with arrows through them. Allie even attempted a picture of Mr. Stubbs's skeleton. The sentiment read, *Happy Valentine's Day from the Three Musketeers.* They each signed their name, and Sharon glued a picture of a pirate on the front.

"Now, that's more like it," Frances said, giving it the thumbs-up.

"I agree," Allie said, going back to work on Mrs. Hemmett's card. "He wouldn't dare throw that in the trash." Allie couldn't wait to see the look on Todd's face when he saw their masterpiece.

Ten minutes later, Allie's mom showed up at the door. "Bedtime, girls."

"Hey, Mom! Look at this cool Valentine we made for Todd Fisher." She handed it to her mom to inspect.

"Well done. Maybe I'll copy this for your dad's Valentine's card." The girls laughed. "Now, bedtime."

"But we haven't finished all our cards yet," Allie said.

"In the morning. Hair brushed, teeth cleaned, and prayers," Mrs. Whitman said as she stepped to the doorway.

"Yes, ma'am," Frances and Sharon said together as Allie nodded. They put the caps on the paste jar and glue bottle, then went off to complete their pre-bedtime routines. When the girls returned and snuggled into bed, Mrs. Whitman kissed Allie on her forehead and turned off the light.

"Good night, Musketeers."

The girls giggled.

After her mom left, the girls started whispering about school, and friends, and Girl Scouts, and Christmas gifts.

"I can't believe you got the Barbie nurse doll for Christmas," Sharon said to Frances. "That doll just came out."

"I know," Frances whispered back. "My dad got it for me. I think he wants me to become a nurse or something."

"You'd make a good nurse," Sharon said.

"Really?"

"Yeah. You're really kind and smart."

"Thanks, Sharon." Frances yawned.

"I mean it."

"And what do you think I'll be?" Allie questioned.

"A world-famous reporter, of course," Sharon said.

"Of course," Frances agreed. "Some sort of writer with all the big words you know."

Allie nudged both of them with her elbows. "You guys are teasing me!"

"No, we're not!" they whispered back. The three started giggling and then shushed themselves into silence.

Sharon yawned. "I'm going to be a mom."

"I'm gonna be a mom, too," Frances said simply. "I'm going to have lots and lots of kids."

"I want to be a mom," Allie confirmed.

"But we are not going to be weird," Sharon added.

"Of course not," Frances said with another yawn.

"And our kids will all turn out perfect, and go to fancy colleges..." Sharon said, the end of her words drifting off.

"...and marry really smart people," Frances added.

Her friends fell silent after that, leaving Allie with her drifting thoughts—thoughts about all the moms she knew and how it was a really tough job. You could cook great meals, and help with homework, and take your kids to church and they still might turn out to be hoodlums. You didn't have much control. Maybe all you could do was teach them good stuff, love them, not have favorites, and let them fall sometimes and bump their heads. Like Trudy said, sometimes people had problems so they could love God more.

In her dreams that night, Allie was walking through a beautiful meadow of green grass. Walking in front of her was Mrs. Turner in her maid's uniform and her son, Mike. Allie was confused because Mike was walking along as though the accident had never happened. Allie's family was behind her, laughing and chattering away. Trudy was talking with a clear voice and saying very smart things. Soon the travelers reached a grassy, flower-covered hill, where a ton of other people were sitting listening to Jesus. She saw Mr. Nessen sitting with Todd Fisher, while Sharon and Frances handed them Valentine's Day cards. She waved at Mrs. Hemmett, who was helping Paul tie wind chimes onto a small cross. She turned and noticed that Mrs. Fisher was seated right next to Jesus, listening intently to His every word. Jesus looked up and gave Allie a smile and a wave. Allie was surprised that He'd seen her in the big crowd of people—and then it didn't seem surprising at all. She sat down next to an old man mending a net, and they started chatting about fish and loaves...and whales.

"Allie? Allie. Wake up," someone was saying from far away. The same someone was poking her. "Allie, wake up." Allie grunted and opened her eyes a slit. She found Sharon smiling at her.

"What?"

"Wake up, sleepyhead. Your mom's calling us for breakfast."

"And it smells delicious," Frances added.

Allie sat up and stretched. "I was having such a good dream." She took a deep breath. "Ahhh...splendiferous," she said with a grin. "Waffles and sausages!"

Frances and Sharon both threw a pillow at her.

"Hey! What was that for?"

"Splendiferous?" Frances giggled "That's certainly one of your big words."

"And it fits the occasion perfectly," Allie said, getting out of bed and putting on her glasses. "Last one to breakfast is a rotten egg!"

"Well, that would be you two cracked little eggs, now, wouldn't it?" Sharon laughed as she jostled with Allie and Frances to be the first one out the bedroom door.

Waffles and sausages make everything better, Allie thought as she ran down the stairs to breakfast.

Waffles, sausages, friends and family, and Jesus.